Also by Clayton Smith

Apocalypticon

Death and McCootie

PANTS ON FIRE

A COLLECTION OF LIES

Copyright © 2013 by Clayton Smith

All rights reserved. Except as permitted under the U.S. Copyright Act of 1976, no part of this publication may be reproduced, distributed, or transmitted in any form or by any means, or stored in a database or retrieval system, without the prior written permission of the publisher.

Dapper Press
www.dapperpress.com
201 W. Millers Road
Des Plaines, IL 60016

Cover design by Emir Orucevic

Printed in the United States of America

ISBN 978-0-9898068-1-7 (pbk.)

For the Matthew McConaughey of ten years from now.

PANTS ON FIRE

A COLLECTION OF LIES

by Clayton Smith

TABLE OF LIES

The Mustache	1
The Death (or Life) of Hattie Dunweather	2
Stranded	16
The Pepper Thief	20
Mirrored	26
In the Cards	32
Hugs or Drugs	43
Cold Feet	47
The Amazing Brutillo	52
The Castle Dim	65
The Saloon at the Edge of Gehenna	77
Pratfall	109
Transcript #371	114
American Sideshow	119
The Rapture and Charlie Gumphrey	123
The Sandalman Song	132
Clarence	141
The World, with Roger Blink	147

The Mustache

There is no story called "The Mustache." The cover of this book is a lie.

The Death (or Life) of Hattie Dunweather

Death came a bit early for Hattie Dunweather, at least in her estimation. At the age of 37, she had led a rather healthy lifestyle and had taken reasonably good care of herself. She ate well (no husband to insist on rich foods), had excellent blood pressure (no in-laws), had never broken a single bone in her body (no siblings), did not smoke (healthy fear of asthma), drank only rarely (birthdays and holidays), and, on the whole, looked and felt several years her junior (no children to expedite gray hairs). Despite the lack of a regular workout routine, she was in good shape and had never paid much heed to diets, trend or otherwise, because she never had need of them, and, in fact, could best be described as "bookish," physically as well as mentally. It should be noted, however, that Hattie had a weakness, as many people do, and her weakness, should she be forced under the penalty of law to disclose such a thing (under what circumstances, I cannot possibly fathom), she would have to confess was a nice, warm slice of mincemeat pie.

For those readers mystified by the concept of a pie constructed chiefly of shredded meat, do not despair. It is not a particularly popular treat, nor is it particularly common, and the chances of you being forced to eat a slice to maintain civility at a family gathering are slim. Mincemeat is decidedly British in its nature and can therefore be disregarded entirely where most civilized palates are concerned. (Perhaps I should note here – as a dutiful narrator might – that it was not this fetish for meat pies that led to Hattie's untimely brush with death, though that is an entirely rational assumption that, if you arrived at it, requires no justification.)

But apart from her one weakness, Hattie was a most well-balanced woman, physically, mentally, and emotionally, if not quite socially. (I refer the reader to my earlier description of her as "bookish.") It came as quite a surprise, then, when Death himself came knocking at her door one fine spring morning.

(Well, to be more accurate, he rang the doorbell. Opportunity may knock, but Death always rings, for he is perfectly aware that sometimes even the hardest of door poundings may go unheard from within, particularly when there is a vacuum running.) It came as quite a surprise, then, when Death himself rang her doorbell one fine spring morning. It was a Wednesday, but it was a holiday, and Hattie was spending her day off from the local library (bookish) by curling up on her favorite understuffed sofa with her newest purchase – a dime-store romance novel featuring bare-chested, oiled-down pirates ("bookish" need not always be confused with "literary") – and one of her two cats, the calico one named Mimsy. Mr. Fox, the wayward orange tabby, was, alas, nowhere to be found. On the fictional good ship Lovelorn, a particularly muscled pirate named Frederick was in the process of swashbuckling his already scant clothing to tatters when the doorbell chimed its happy tune – some quaint bastardization of *Ave Maria* that cheered Hattie each time it had cause to play, which was not very often. She held her page in the book captive with a generic cat food coupon, tossed the unwilling Mimsy to the floor, and trotted across the living room to the front door. Because a surprise visitor is always either very welcome or very unwelcome, she peeped her eye through the peephole so as to ascertain into which category her guest fell. Sure enough, as the reader already knows, there stood the pallid figure of Death.

She guessed it was death by the flowing, black-hooded robe he wore and the long, blade-ended staff he carried. Under other circumstances, she might have thought him nothing more than a very somber wheat farmer, but she had been introduced just three weeks earlier to this very figure though a certain Ingmar Bergman film acquired from the library's video rental center (35 cents for three days, and not quite worth it in her estimation). But she'd been wrong before, and she felt it best to acquire absolute certainty before denying admittance, for she was a hearty supporter of our country's natural resources and the Midwestern men and women who tended them, and it would sadden her greatly to turn such a farmer away due to mistaken identity. And so she cautiously asked, "Who is it?" with just the right mixture of warmth and skepticism befitting the occasion.

Death began fiddling with his robes. "Ahm..." he said, very much aware of people's aversions to admitting entrance to beings such as himself. "Ahm... my name's... Donald." Yes, that was a clever lie. *Well done, Death*, he thought.

"And what's your occupation, Donald?" Hattie asked shrewdly from the other side of the barrier. This was a question that Death had not quite counted on. His countenance fell, or it would have, had he a countenance. Ethereal beings, such as they are, actually have very few facial features and rarely know what to do with the ones they possess. "Ahm..." he said again. He was not terribly good at extemporaneous speaking. "Well... ah... look, I'm not the Grim Reaper, if that's what you're thinking."

Aha! thought Hattie. *Now I have him!* "If you're not the Grim Reaper, then why did you automatically assume I pegged you as the Grim Reaper?"

"Well... ahm..." *Think! Think! Think!* "I suppose most people just see the robe and think of Death."

"It's probably because of that Ingmar Bergman film," said Hattie.

"What?" said Death.

"I said it's probably because of that Ingmar Bergman film!" The door was acting as an unfortunate conversation muffler, but aside from that, this little *tête-à-tête* was invigorating! This was the most rousing row Hattie had had in quite some time, and having the conversational upper hand over an immortal was an enlivening experience. Hattie decided to push on. "If you're not the Grim Reaper, then what are you?"

"Umm…" Death gave himself a once-over. "A very somber wheat farmer?"

Drat, thought Hattie. She contemplated her next move, and while she did so, Death took her silence as a sign of (surprising) victory. "Yes!" he continued. "I am a very somber wheat farmer. You see my farming implement here, and this very dour robe."

Hattie gritted her teeth. How had he managed to turn the tables? "You *may* be a very somber wheat farmer," she conceded. "But you also might not be. How can I know for sure?"

"Well!" scoffed Death, feigning injury to his soul. "As a Midwestern farmer dedicated to tending America's naturally wheaty resources, I am appalled that you would consider me false!"

"Yes, I can understand that," Hattie admitted. "If you *are* a very somber wheat farmer, I'll feel just awful for doubting you. But, of course, if you're really Death, that's just the sort of thing you would say to get me to lower my defenses, isn't it?"

"Is it?"

"Isn't it?"

"*Is it?*"

"*Isn't it?*"

Death scratched his head. This was getting him nowhere. He tried another tactic: total non-sequiturism. "Can I come in?"

"No, I don't think so."

My, but this cursed woman was sharp. Nothing could throw her off her game! "Well, why not?" he demanded.

"I think you're Death," she reasoned, face still pressed flat against the peephole. "If you were a wheat farmer, your clothes would be much dirtier."

Drat.

"Okay. You got me. I'm not a very somber wheat farmer."

"Ah *ha*! I knew it! You have to get up pretty early to fool ol' Hattie Dunweather," Hattie said smartly. "Say, what's that in your other hand?" she asked, squinting through the glass.

"Oh, this? It's a… it's a chessboard," Death replied.

"Ah!" The old blood was really pumping now! "That seals it! Death had a chessboard in that movie, too! Now there's no one else you could possibly be!" Death found himself rather befuddled by this statement. "So what if he's got a chessboard in the movie?" he said in consternation. "That doesn't prove anything!"

"It most certainly does!" she exclaimed. "Why else would you be holding one in your hand? You want to play chess with me then slice me up!"

"What the hell are you talking about?" Death exploded. "I don't have a chessboard!"

"Yes you do! You just said you did, and I can see it right there!"

"No, you dolt, I said clipboard, not chessboard! *Clip*board!" And as he wagged it toward the peephole, she saw with no small amount of embarrassment that it *was* a clipboard, and the muffling of the door had allowed her to hear "chessboard."

"Well, why do you need a clipboard?" she asked, trying to regain some footing in this battle of wits. "It's your list of souls to claim, I suppose?"

Actually, this was exactly what the clipboard was used for.

"That's not what it's used for at all!" cried Death. "It's… it's… ahm… I'm…" Then, inspiration! "I'm a research analyst!"

"A research analyst?"

"Yes, a research analyst! I'm taking a survey!"

Hmm, thought Hattie. In her job at the library, she was required to occasionally survey library patrons regarding the quality of their individual book-finding experiences. These surveys usually ended in abrupt, impolite altercations borne of snippy retorts from patrons who just wanted to be left alone, *thankyouverymuch*. As such, she had a special sympathy for fellow surveyors of all kinds, and she certainly did not want to turn this man away empty-handed if he really *was* taking a survey. Curses, but the game was still on. "If you're a research analyst, why did you say you were a wheat farmer?"

"Oh." Death shuffled his feet. "Ahm… oh! I thought that if you knew I was a research analyst, maybe you wouldn't open the door. People don't really like opening their doors for survey takers. Do they?" he asked, genuinely wondering if he had that right.

Hattie nodded slowly. "Yes, that's certainly true." She could understand that, all right. "What sort of survey is it?" Death had, of course, anticipated this question.

"A very important survey," he answered, "I'm taking a poll of this neighborhood to see which is the more preferred type of flooring: hardwood, tile, or carpet. Might I come in and have a look?"

"I don't know," replied a wary Hattie. "That still doesn't explain the sickle."

"Oh. Yes. Well. It's for… ahm… well… protection! Against… you know… dogs, and… and whatnot." He held his breath and winced.

"And… and against the people who get angry when you ask them to take a quick survey because they don't understand just how hard you have to work to get a few answers, and they have no concern for your feelings whatsoever, even to the point of laughing at you when their mockery and dissent turns you to tears?" Hattie suggested. She was breathing very heavily now; he had touched on a nerve very near her heart.

"Yes!" he agreed happily. "Yes, exactly!"

"Those monsters!"

"Brutes!"

"Yes. Well." Hattie considered her options. Her heart bled for the black-clad pollster outside her door, but there was still a chance, however slight, that he was really Death after all. Could she afford to take that chance? "Listen. Why don't I just tell you? It's hardwood. My whole house is covered in hardwood."

Death shook his head. "I'm sorry, no good. I need to see it for myself. Verify the results, you know?"

Hattie bit at her lip nervously. What would pirate captain Frederick do in this situation? He'd probably do something immensely shirtless. Hattie fanned her cheeks. "Oh, I know! Listen. I'll tap on it with my foot, and you can hear for yourself."

"What?"

"I said, I'll tap on it with my foot, and you can hear it for yourself!" She tapped on the wood floor beneath her, quite loudly, in fact, and this was very clearly heard through the door, and it was very clearly a wood floor.

"No good!" said Death. "You might very well be tapping on a *piece* of wood on the floor to try to fool me. I have very strict supervisors. They demand complete verification. I had better check for myself." Hattie considered this. If he really were a pollster, he was a very shrewd one, and she felt she could learn much from his style of surveying. "Well then… why don't you just look in through the window?" She reached out and tapped the glass of the tall, thin window bordering the right side of the door to show him where to look. "Still no good! I've got… ahm… cataracts," said the quick-thinking reaper. Hattie caught her breath. *Oh, the poor man!* She had astigmatism herself, and she knew how troubling vision problems could be. She didn't want to make him feel bad about his handicap by insisting he try anyway, but still, she just couldn't take the chance of letting him in! She needed time to think.

"Look," she said, "why don't you come back in a little bit? Say… an hour, maybe?"

"What for?" Death cried.

"I need to… to tidy up! If I'm going to let someone into my house, it needs to be clean."

"Oh, I don't mind a mess, really." *There'll be a new mess when I'm through*, he thought cheerily.

"I'm sorry, I just couldn't allow it. I'll need an hour. Maybe two."

"I'm sorry, I really don't think that'll work for me," said Death, a bit too testily, perhaps. "I'm on a tight schedule, you see." Hattie thought about this. It could be true for both pollsters and soul harvesters. It gave her no clue as to his real identity.

"I'm sorry. I've made up my mind. You'll just have to wait."

Death grumbled a few expletives at the door, which dutifully filtered the language for the comparatively pure ears listening on the other side. This was what they called "a dead end." He needed a new approach. He needed a plan. He stepped from Hattie's porch and paced in front of her house, absentmindedly crisscrossing the lawn, leaving a jagged path of dead grass in his wake. Had Hattie still been standing at her peephole, she might have noticed this very recently departed swatch of grass and then been entirely satisfied as to her would-be houseguest's true nature. However, as fate would have it, she had peeled her face away from the door (nursing it back to health, having numbed it by pressing it against the peephole for so long) and returned to her sofa and to Mimsy, missing the brown trail of death altogether.

Meanwhile, Death had struck upon an idea. It wasn't a very good idea, but it was *an* idea, and those were in short supply at this point. He pulled out his cell phone and hit speed dial 3.

Twenty minutes later, a rusted-out jalopy sputtered its way to a half-stop, half-death-gasp in Hattie's driveway. Death, who had at some point in the interim noticed the trail of destruction he was wreaking on the lawn, was sitting on the sidewalk, wringing his robe in his hands. He leapt up when he saw the familiar rust bucket and tried not to look too anxious. The driver cut the already dying engine and opened the door. Out stepped a man who, dear reader, can only be accurately described as "sickly." His pencil-thin arms were perilously connected to a pair of knobby shoulders, and his skeletal hands helplessly clutched a bumpy chest, covered, thankfully, by a tattered, oil-stained blue shirt. Had it not been hidden from sight, the eyes of any nosy onlookers would have undoubtedly been drawn to the man's mountainous rib cage, which protruded horribly above the stomach. His hair, thin wisps of flaxen gray, clung to his scaly scalp for dear life, lest the lightest wind set them free. And he was ghostly pale, from the brow above his sunken eyes to the toes of his yellow, corned feet, which shuffled along lamely in worn rubber sandals.

All in all, he certainly looked his part.

"Where have you been?" Death demanded with a stomp of his foot. "I'm *way* behind schedule!"

"Sorry," sniffed the drowsy old man. "Don't move as fast as I used to." He hobbled his way to the rear passenger-side door and pulled it open with great effort. He hunched his sickly body over and somehow managed to hold his bones together as he reached in and drew out a small white cardboard box. He turned and offered it to Death.

"It had better be a good one," the reaper snapped, snatching the proffered box from his friend's shaking hands. "And it better be in one piece!"

"'Course it's in one piece," hacked the other man. "What do you think I am?"

"I think, my friend, that you are the living embodiment of Famine and will stop at very little to have a bite of something, *anything*, since you haven't tasted food in several million years."

"Yeah," said the old man, wiping his sleeve across his mouth as he coughed up something brownish and thick, "but I got my pride. Besides, I know what you had put in that thing. I ain't that stupid."

"Yes, well, bully you." Death turned and ran up the walk to Hattie's door, small white cardboard box in hand. Again, he prodded the doorbell. He waited, rather impatiently, as Hattie padded her way to the door. A small eclipse overtook the peephole as she covered it from the inside with a wary eye.

"Who is it?"

"Oh, come off it," said Death. "You know who it is."

"Oh, it's you."

"Of course it's me. Have you decided to let me in?"

"No, I'm still thinking."

"Well," said Death, not too smugly, he hoped, "that's a great shame. Looks like I'll have to eat this pie out on your porch all by myself." He nodded at the little white box. Hattie's interest was instantly piqued.

"Pie, you say?" She watched Death pretend to ignore her through the peephole. "What kind of pie?"

"Oh, probably not the kind you'd be interested in," replied Death. "It's not a very popular kind of pie."

"Try me."

"It's just, you see, I have this thing for mincemeat pies."

"Mincemeat pies!" Hattie couldn't suppress her excitement. It had been days, literally *days*, since her last meaty treat, and, as the reader will recall, a good mincemeat pie (or even a bad one, for that matter) was Hattie's one true weakness. "That wouldn't happen to *be* a mincemeat pie, would it? In that little box of yours?"

"Oh, it might," said Death coyly. "I guess there's only one way to tell." At this point, he very dramatically opened the lid of the small white cardboard box and peeked in, then made an astonished "Oh!" sound, as if he had not quite expected his good fortune. "Why, as a matter of fact, it *is* a mincemeat pie!"

Hattie's mother, however, had raised no fool. "Hold it up to the window," she said. "Let me see for myself."

Death stole a moment of silent inner joy. So his files, the ones clipped to his clipboard (that did not, incidentally, resemble anything remotely like a survey of any sort), hadn't been wrong after all. The woman really *did* have a penchant for these disgusting, decidedly British treats that can be entirely disregarded where most civilized palates are concerned. He held the box up to the vertical window next to the door with a wry smile, just long enough for Hattie to see that it was, in fact, a mincemeat pie, and then pulled it away with great relish and made as if to gobble it all up himself, right then and there. "Wait, wait!" cried Hattie through the door.

She felt very strongly that she should do something to make herself the owner of that delectable little treat, but she still did not trust the black-robed man outside her door. She stamped her foot in desperation. Oh, he was a clever one, he was! But then, as she peeped out onto her porch, she was struck by a marvelous idea! "That man! That man lying near my driveway. Do you see him?"

Death turned. "Lying ne--? Oh, for crying out loud," he huffed. Famine had collapsed on the sidewalk right near Hattie's mailbox. A woman with a bag full of fresh produce sidestepped him. As she passed the prostrate figure, much to her astonishment and chagrin, her leafy lettuce dropped into sickly brown rags, and her tangerines began instantly to rot. Death smacked his forehead with the palm of his hand, nearly taking his head off with his own scythe as he did.

"What, you mean *him*?"

"Yes, him. Go pick him up and send him in with the pie."

"You have got to be kidding me."

"What's that?"

"I said, you have got to be kidding me! Look at him! He looks like the crypt keeper. How come he gets to go into the house and I don't?"

"He has kind eyes," Hattie said defiantly.

"Kind eyes! Ugh." Hattie watched with glee as Death huffed off back down the walkway and pulled the thin, sickly man up off the ground. The two men conferred with very animated gestures (actually, only Death's gestures were animated; the other man's were quite slow and looked rather painful). Eventually, Death shoved the box of pie into the other man's arms and pushed him toward the front door with his worn rubber sandals sliding the whole way up the walk.

The sickly man, who looked like he could do with a pie or two himself, nervously approached the door and rang the bell. Hattie dispensed with the usual formalities and jerked open the door. She grabbed the old man by the wrist and yanked him inside, then slammed the door quickly behind him so Death couldn't sneak his way in. She turned and sized up the man in her foyer. He could use some food, all right. Perhaps she'd give him something from her icebox. A bit of cheese, or a grape. Certainly not any of the pie. That was her treat alone.

Hmm, she thought. *Strange.* She hadn't been particularly peckish, not even when the black-robed man had shown her the pie, but now that she was so close to it, she felt very hungry, very hungry indeed. *Extremely* hungry. *Ravenously* hungry. Pains cramped in around her stomach, severe pains, as if she hadn't eaten in weeks, nay, months, maybe even *years*, and... and she needed that pie.

But starvation or no starvation, first she needed to gloat.

Hattie turned back to the door for one last little jab at the maybe Grim Reaper/maybe wheat farmer/maybe survey taker outside. "Here I go," she called happily through the door. "I'm going to enjoy this delicious mincemeat pie all by myself and leave none for anyone else!" And, convinced that she had dealt some sort of deathblow to her unhappy pursuer, she turned back to Famine and the pie.

But there was no more pie. What stood in its place was an empty pie box, a Mimsy, and a Famine (who was now, on a very slight scale, less famished), the latter two creatures having ravaged the pie clean in a fit of weakness. Famine looked up from the mess of crumbs with bleary, red-rimmed eyes.

"I'm sorry, miss," he said, without managing to look or sound too terribly sorry. "I don't know what come over me. I just ain't had a meal in millions of years, and I just—I just—" And he burped, and then he fell over dead. And then so did the cat.

Hattie stood over them, her mouth agape. Should she be angry that they ate her pie or shocked that they had just died? Angry, she decided.

"Look!" she screamed, going to the door. "That man there just ate my entire pie! All by himself!" she lied, intentionally not mentioning the cat, because why get into those feelings of betrayal now? There'd be time enough. "And he left none for me! Not a crumb! Now you tell me, just what am I supposed to do with that?"

Death, who had been cleaning beneath his fingernails with the tip of his scythe, closed his eyes and smashed his head against the dull side of the blade. "He *ate* the *pie*?"

"I should say so! The whole thing in one gulp, I imagine! And now, just look at him. Look at him! He's dead! Choked on it, I guess!" Of course, Famine had not choked on the pie. He had been poisoned by the pie, which had been injected with said poison on Death's orders. "Oh, and he killed Mimsy!" she fibbed again, because, seriously, why even *try* dealing with that emotional grab bag right now? Death, having no idea what a "Mimsy" was, felt no pang of remorse for indirectly causing the cat's demise. He did, however, have a great deal of concern for the death of Famine, as it posed a formidable problem. Not only did it hamper his plan to obtain the soul of one Hattie Dunweather, but, looking at the bigger picture, it certainly threw a monkey wrench in the works as far as Armageddon was concerned. There were to be four horsemen, *four* – one of whom was now dead, deceased, expired, completely spoilt not twenty feet away from him. What now? And oh, what would Pestilence say? Pestilence, always so snippy anyway, always going on about "Boil me that soup," and "Get me my blanket," and "I'll catch my death," and "Stop that racket, my head is pounding." He was going to be an absolute nightmare about the whole thing. And War. War wouldn't be much better. He'd make a whole campaign of it. *Criminy*, thought Death. *What a kerfluckle.* Armageddon wasn't scheduled for quite some time, of course, but eventually, oh, eventually it was going to be a problem.

And still, with the fate of the demise of the world at stake, the mad Hattie droned on and on about her stupid lost pie. "How dare you taunt a poor, single woman with a meat pie, only to instruct your partner—yes, I believe now that he was your *partner*, a clever game, the two of you run!—to devour it at once! I don't care if you *are* a very somber wheat farmer! There is now *no way* you're getting in this house!"

And, of course, it was true. Nothing Death could have said or done would have made her open that door. Not that it mattered much anymore, anyway. Certainly not in the grand scheme of things, and, as he was beginning to suspect, probably not really in the small scheme of things either. Hattie lived a fairly inconspicuous life. Went virtually unnoticed by the general public. Her life or death, when it came right down to it, was really inconsequential – not just to Death, but to the entire planet. Her biggest impact was an ink stamp in a book cover.

So Death, who was now quite preoccupied with much, *much* larger issues (most of them relating to the tongue lashing he was sure to receive from his remaining two cohorts), did the only thing there really was left to do: He left. He simply left. He threw up his hands in defeat, he turned from Hattie's door, and he strode off to his next victim, a Mr. Reginald Pimm, an 87-year-old cancer patient who, Death knew, would be a much easier sell. As for Hattie (who, by the way, after all these years, is *still* angry about the pie that could have been, and, to a somewhat lesser, suppressed degree, about her dead cat), he would return to her on a later circuit, de-soul her at a much later point in life, when she would just open the damn door and be done with it.

Or, he thought, as he walked a wide, spiteful arc through her temporarily green lawn, perhaps… just perhaps… well, perhaps he wouldn't return for her at all.

And that, dear reader, is *exactly* what he did.

Stranded

Why didn't my father teach me how to change a damn tire? I know why. Because he was too busy futzing around with that bottle-blonde tramp, that's why. This is all his fault. How embarrassing. My *sister* knows how to change a tire. I've seen her do it. And she has an IQ of 90. I have an Ivy League degree. So why the hell don't I know how to change this tire? I could've bought fifty brand-new cars with the money I spent on that stupid education. Why didn't I just do that? Then I wouldn't have to change this tire, I could just change *cars*. And why didn't I take shop in high school, damn it? Christ, why did I never watch "Dukes of Hazzard?"

This is also Marlena's fault. Why the hell does she live so far from the rest of the human race? Who lives off gravel roads anymore? Seriously. Gravel roads? I thought they only existed on re-runs of "The Waltons." Haven't these hicks ever heard of asphalt? They can use tar to feather minorities, but they can't slop a little on their roads. I hate the country. I *hate* the country. And I hate this damn road. What's it called? St. Paul's Road? Probably because you have to pray to him every time you take it so you don't end up with a razor-sharp rock stuck in your tire in the middle of the goddamn gravel dirt-ass road!

Why is there *no one* coming along to help? I've been here for half an hour! Shouldn't someone have passed through by now? Do these people even *own* cars, or do they drive tractors and horse carts through the woods? Of course, if someone *did* come, I'd have a whole new problem. "Excuse me, could you help me? I'm not very masculine at all, and I don't know how to change this tire. I live in the city, see…" A comment like that would probably get me shot out here. Which would actually be just fine, because if I have to sit here in the middle of the sticks in the pitch black for ten more seconds, I'm going to lose my fucking mind.

God, this place is creepy. Haven't they ever heard of streetlights? Do they even *have* electricity? Maybe Marlena uses candles. Who'd want to run power lines out this far? Ugh, and it's so damn *quiet*! There's not a single noise out here except my goddamned hazard lights clicking on and off. *Thunk-thonk, thunk-thonk*. I'd lose my mind in this quiet. I think I *am* losing my mind in this quiet. I mean, there isn't one single noise—wait. There was a noise. What the hell was that? What the hell *was* that? A twig snapping? Why would a twig be snapping? Maybe someone's coming. Maybe it's a wild boar. Oh God, do wild boars even exist? Or are they imaginary, like narwhals? Forest narwhals? Maybe I should get inside the car. And lock the doors.

This is so stupid. I really am losing it. All right. Tire. I can do this. I can *do* this! And think how badass it'll be when I tell Marlena the story of how I was late because I had to stop off and change my own tire on the side of the road. Girls love that shit. Okay. I can do this. Let's see. Okay. The tire appears to be held on by these bolts. How the hell do I take these things off? Hold on… maybe if I can grip it just right, I—*nrrugh. Mruupf!* Dammit! Why did I stop going to the gym? It's my trainer's fault for letting me quit.

There it is again. That noise. What the hell *is* that? I swear if I get eaten by a rabid coyote, I am coming straight back and haunting every single racist hick within thirty miles of this place. Holy— there it was again! Okay, it was really close that time. Seriously, something is out here. I'm getting back in the car. Back in the car, back in the car, back in the car, back in the car! *Aaaaand* lock the door. Can animals really smell fear? Dear God, I hope not. I'd smell like a Jew at a Christmas pageant by now. You know what? It's probably not a rabid animal at all. It's probably a rabid redneck. Someone let him off his leash. His name's probably Bubba, he has a gallon of tobacco juice sloshing around his mouth, and even if he kills me, he won't be able to eat me because he only has two teeth.

This is so stupid.

Yes, I know, stop mocking me, cell phone. I *know* you're not getting any service! I *realize* that! Thank you *so much* for your goddamn help!

Why the hell am I out here? I barely even know this woman. She probably lives under a woodpile with her crazy Aunt Flo. If I'd known she lived this far out, I never would have agreed to a third date. Also, shouldn't she be out looking for me? Doesn't she care about me at all? This is never going to work out. You know why? Because I'm going to die out here. I'm going to die in this car, with its flat tire, and my epitaph is going to be horrifically insulting. I just know it. I wonder if anyone will come to the funeral. I wonder if Marlena will come. I think it's the least she could do. I wonder if she'd bring her Aunt Flo. She'd have to pull the sticks out of Flo's hair and teach her how to walk in shoes. So probably not.

What was that? Okay, that was *not* a twig snap. That was a crunch. Like… like gravel. Under a foot. Or a hoof. Or a giant paw. There it is again! Dear Christ, what *is* that? I don't see anybody. Wait. Is that—? Something is walking this way. I can hear it. Crunching closer and closer. Oh my God! What if it's someone with a gun? They all have guns out here. I've seen "Deliverance." Guns and pigs. Dammit! What was I thinking, turning my hazard lights on? I'm like a fucking lighthouse! I should turn them off. Right? Yes. Right. Okay. Okay. Off. Now. Don't make a sound. Maybe he can't see me. Blend into the dark. Why did I come here, why did I come here, why did I—dear God, it's getting closer! Quiet, now. Don't breathe. Don't breathe. Don't—

Oh my God. It is a man… with… with yellow eyes? *Why the fuck does he have yellow eyes?* Holy shit, and he *does* have a gun!

Wait. No… not a gun… oh Jesus. Holy shit! A machete! Oh God. Is he—? Oh God. Oh God! He is! He's covered in blood!

Goddammit. I hate the country.

The Pepper Thief

In hindsight, the extended family should not have been invited to Sunday dinner. It's not that they weren't enjoyable in their own individual ways. It's just that most of them were utterly insane and should probably have been under regular, professional supervision.

Still. Tradition was tradition.

Evidence of the theory of family insanity had piled up quite heavily in recent months. There was the crayon fiasco with Aunt Clare, the wax-fruit mix-up with little Lenny, the cotton ball mishap with Great Uncle Roy, the marble trauma with Ricky the poodle, and the forever-infamous pudding incident with Cousin Steve, whose motor functions really couldn't possibly be *that* bad, no matter how awful his accident with the badger had been. And, of course, there were others, but many of them could be (and were) played off as minor incidents and mistakes. But that particular Sunday, it became very clear to Marsha Canfield that she had to either start committing her family members to the asylum or get busy committing herself.

Most of the day had gone smoothly, and by the time dinner was served, Marsha had felt foolishly optimistic about the chances of finishing the monthly ritual with minimal problems. This illusion did not last long.

"Where's the pepper?" she asked, scanning the table. "Has anyone seen the pepper?"

Asking this question was a mistake.

Aunt Clare looked up from her turkey and eyed Marsha suspiciously. "You lost the pepper?" she asked harshly.

"I wouldn't say it's lost," said Marsha, her face flushing with heat. *God, here we go...* "It's just not on the table. Not to worry, I'll go get it."

"Well," huffed Aunt Clare. "I would certainly take more care if it were *my* table being set." This was a typical comment made by Clare, whose favorite pastime was to criticize others for the actions she had no intention of carrying out herself. Marsha shook it off with a roll of her shoulders and was about to return to the kitchen in search of the wayward pepper grinder when a gnarled old finger thrust itself into the air at the other end of the table.

"Ah *ha!*" shouted Grandpa Joe, who had read far too many Agatha Christie novels in his day. "Missing pepper, eh? Missing pepper, you say?! Something's... *afoot!*" He closed his outstretched finger into his palm, making a fist, and slammed it down on the table. Silverware went scattering across the cloth, and little Lenny's glass of milk tipped over, spilling its contents onto his full plate. Lenny, who was a very slow child indeed, thought perhaps his turkey was bleeding white blood and began screaming at the thought of being served a freshly killed, raw piece of bird flesh. He jumped back from his chair and fled, screaming and flailing, from the room in terror. He crashed into the wall of the living room adjacent to the dining room and thumped to the ground, unconscious.

"Oh, for crying out loud!" said Marsha. "It's not missing! There's nothing afoot! It's in the kitchen!"

"Don't you try to pacify me!" screamed Grandpa Joe, wagging a finger at her. "I know when something's afoot! And something is definitely afoot!"

"Stop saying that," said Cousin Steve, sloshing a spoonful of potatoes into his mouth. "That's not even a word."

"What isn't a word?" asked Great Aunt Bernice.

"Afoot."

"It most certainly *is* a word!" shrieked Grandpa Joe. "It's the best word, and I shall continue to use it until something is no longer... *afoot!*" He slammed his fist down on the table again. The gravy boat tipped over, and steaming hot sausage gravy spilled onto Great Uncle Roy's crotch. He didn't seem to notice.

"Look, everyone just calm down," said Marsha in a very practiced tone. "I'll get the pepper. Everything will be fine."

"No! It's not fine! The case must be solved!" Grandpa Joe pushed himself from the table, knocking over his chair in the process and sprawling to the floor in a flash of limbs and corduroy. "Who did that?" he yelled from the floor, swinging his fists up at an invisible adversary. "Who tripped me?"

Marsha shook her head, sighed deeply, and went into the kitchen to search for the pepper.

Meanwhile, little Lenny, who was still quite unconscious, was in the process of dreaming about a newborn kitty named Herbert. In his dream, little Lenny loved Herbert very much, and Herbert loved little Lenny, too. Lenny found that he was able to communicate his deepest wishes to Herbert by speaking in the small kitten's native tongue. Unfortunately, stupid little Lenny, who was never very good with animals, dreamt that Herbert, and indeed all cats, spoke in quacks instead of meows.

Out in the waking world, Grandpa Joe, who was still on the floor, pricked up his ears as the sound of quacks came from the next room. "Wait! Everyone! Be quiet!" he cried. The sound of a duck was very clear. "Son of a—it's a *duck!*" he yelled. Grandpa Joe had come out on the wrong end of a bad run-in with a duck not three weeks ago in one of his addle-brained hallucinations, for which he'd stopped taking his medication, and he had looked forward to revenge ever since. He rolled himself onto his stomach like a frenzied turtle, then pushed up from the ground and ran into the living room, carving fork in hand, ready for round two with the devious little water fowl. When he reached the room, however, the duck had fled, probably in terror, and all he saw was his nimrod little grandson, napping in the corner.

Marsha came back into the dining room, pepper grinder in hand, to find Grandpa Joe's overturned seat empty. "Where's dad?" she demanded of Cousin Steve.

"He went after a duck," said Steve, while trying to cut his turkey with short, choppy movements that resulted in a spray of bird juice splattering everything in a three-foot radius.

"Oh, dear Lord," said Marsha. "He didn't go after the neighbor's ducks, did he?" Cousin Steve, who was very eager to redeem himself in the eyes of Grandpa Joe after the forever-infamous pudding incident, threw his silverware across the table (the fork ricocheting off Great Uncle Roy's forehead, which he didn't seem to notice), and jumped to his feet. "Next door?" he cried. And he bolted from the room, shouting heroic nonsense about honor avenged. These cries came to a brief halt, however, as he misjudged the distance to the front door and smashed directly into it, face-first. He rebounded surprisingly quickly, yanked at the knob, and bounded out the door in the direction of the neighbor's house.

Marsha pulled a flask out of her pocket and started swigging.

Grandpa Joe came back into the room rubbing his hands together. "It was the duck!" he said. "The duck stole the pepper! There's no question."

"Dad," said Marsha, pocketing the flask, "the duck did not steal the pepper. The pepper is right here."

"Well, it may be there *now*," said Grandpa Joe. "But you know how ducks are! I think… we all know… how ducks are." He spat onto the carpet to prove how displeased he was with the imaginary duck. Ricky the poodle crept over to the wet, lumpy spot on the shag and began lapping at it. Grandpa Joe shooed him away with his toe. The stupid dog was ruining his moment.

Just then, the front door slammed open with great force, because it had been kicked in by Cousin Steve, who had no time for doorknobs. The doorjamb splintered, and the glass from the window shattered and crashed to the floor. He crunched over it, oblivious. Under one excited arm he carried a very serene-looking duck. "Here he is, Grandpa Joe!" he exclaimed, presenting the old man with the small, gray fowl. "I got him!"

"Stephen!" shrieked Marsha. "You return Mr. Henderson's duck right this very instant!" Grandpa Joe's eyes grew wide at the sight of the duck, and he lunged at it. "Grandpa! No!" But it was too late. Grandpa Joe seized the duck by the throat and started shaking it violently.

"Thought you could steal the pepper, did you?! Thought you could try darning my socks while I was asleep, did you?! I *wanted* those holes there, you little bastard! *I wanted those holes there!*" He throttled the duck and swung it up and down, *whumping* it on the table. More liquids spilled out of more containers. Grandpa Joe brought the duck down on the surface with greater and greater force, until a cracking sound was heard. With one final blow, the duck's head snapped off in Grandpa's hand, and its little gray body shot through the air, caught Great Aunt Bernice in the head, and sent her rocketing to the floor, only semi-conscious, with half-chewed green beans sticking out of her mouth.

"Grandpa! You broke Mr. Henderson's duck!" Marsha angrily snatched the wooden head out of the old man's shaking hands. "He carved this himself! It took him weeks!" Grandpa Joe gasped.

"Wooden duck!" he exclaimed. His gaze shifted to Cousin Steve. "You brought me a wooden duck?! What are you playing at here, you nitwit?" He grabbed the wooden duck head from Marsha and launched it at Steve. He opened his mouth to protest, and the head shot into his mouth and hit the back of his throat. He started gagging, choking on the smooth piece of wood. He hammered at his diaphragm with his fist, trying to dislodge the wayward mallard head. Marsha gasped in horror and rushed to Steve's aid to administer the Heimlich maneuver. The wooden head was successfully dislodged; it shot out of his mouth and rolled across the carpet and under the table. Ricky the poodle, losing interest in the glob of grandpa's phlegm, padded over to investigate. The smell of turkey-flavored mucus coated the wood, and Ricky scarfed it down. But it caught in his throat, and with a pathetic *squeak*, the dog fell over dead. Great Aunt Bernice, who had a perfect view of Ricky's death from her position on the floor, cried out in anguish, having mistaken Ricky for little Lenny in her semi-conscious confusion and began giving the dog mouth-to-mouth. Grandpa Joe, oblivious to the predicament of the dog, hurled silverware at Cousin Steve, whom he had not forgiven since the forever-infamous pudding incident. Steve ducked away from flying forks and knives, ran straight through the dining room, and dove through the closed window overlooking the backyard, sending glass showering down on the rose garden and falling two stories into a particularly prickly hedgerow. Grandpa Joe ran to the window and continued flinging silverware at him from above, losing cutlery in the mess of shrubbery below.

Marsha retrieved her flask from her pocket and plopped down at the table. She shook the pepper onto her turkey and chased a bite with whiskey. She looked around and surveyed the damage, wondering, not for the first time, if she had been adopted. Only Aunt Clare remained at the table, sitting primly and staring at Marsha with accusing eyes.

"*Well*," she huffed, "this rigmarole *never* happens under *my* watch."

Marsha abandoned the turkey and guzzled from the flask. Aunt Clare will be the first to be committed, she decided. If she were lucky, the others would just kill each other off.

Mirrored

The person in the mirror is a complete stranger. I don't mean that as some hyperbole on the nature of inner reflection. I mean literally. He is a stranger. My reflection looks nothing like me. I guess he has the sameish haircut, but his hair isn't brown. It's black. Jet black. And maybe his nose is as pointy as mine. *Maybe.* But his eyes are wide, not squinty; his ears are way too sharp; he looks like maybe he tans; and his mouth is always sneering. Even when he's frowning, he's sneering. Even when he's yawning, he's sneering. I never sneer. I don't think I even know how. I'm not a sneery person. Some people are sneery people. I'm not sneery. But every time I look in the mirror, there I am, or, rather, there *he* is, sneering away.

I first noticed it about a week ago. I wonder if this is a new development, or if my reflection has never really been my reflection at all. It's ridiculous, I know, but think about it. How well do we really see ourselves? Again, not metaphorically. Literally. How well do we see ourselves? In mirrors, and in photos. The real you and the photographed you never really match up all the way, do they?

I think he knows that I know. At first, of course, he played it off like he was nothing more than a mirror image. He made the same moves I made, and the same basic faces. I raised my left hand; he raised his right hand. I frowned; he frowned. I stuck my tongue out; he stuck his tongue out. But I spent too much time trying to trick him, I guess. Too much time trying to get him to slip up. It's not normal for a person to spend so much time at the mirror. He must have known something was up, because now he doesn't even bother trying. When I come to a mirror, he makes obscene gestures. *I* don't make obscene gestures, you understand. I think they're crude. But he doesn't. He seems to think they're hilarious. Honestly, I don't know why I just didn't stop looking. It's not like he was helping me style my hair or check for zits or anything. Seeing a stranger flip you the bird doesn't exactly do wonders for your hygiene. It really didn't do me any good to keep looking. Force of habit, I guess.

I don't want to get off point here, but I wonder if this happens to anyone else. I'm dying to ask around, but it's not the sort of thing you bring up at dinner. "How was your day today?" "Oh, it was fine. Say, is the person in your mirror a deranged doppelganger?" That's the sort of question that has great disruption potential, I think.

Plus, truth be told, I wasn't overly concerned about it at first. My mirror double could make all the awful gestures he wanted, it wasn't really affecting me. Not on a personal level.

Not until yesterday, that is.

Yesterday, he did something new. When I looked into the foggy bathroom mirror after stepping out of the shower, he wasn't sneering. He was doing something else entirely. Something like a smile, but harsher. A smirk, maybe. He raised one finger, which had been resting somewhere beneath the frame, and he brought it up to the surface of the mirror, on his side, of course. Then he started to draw letters in the steam. It must have been hard; he had to do it backward. But he didn't seem to have too much trouble. When he was done, *I'M GOING TO KILL YOU* was pretty legibly scrawled into the mist. Then he waved, very slowly, and breathed onto the mirror, covering the words and his reflection in fresh steam.

That got me a bit panicked.

I tried to avoid him the rest of the day, but it's not as easy as you'd think. The rearview mirror in the car, the reflection in a puddle, washing your hands after the restroom. It's practically impossible to avoid seeing your reflection altogether. So I caught snippets of him here and there — peripherals, you understand — and every time I did, I could see he was pointing to something in his left hand. I made a near mastery of averting my eyes, so as not to see what he wanted me to see. But damn curiosity, damn it all to hell! I had to know. So at work, I excused myself from my desk and went into the restroom and locked the door behind me. I took a deep breath and peeked one eye up to the mirror. There he stood, that miserable, reflection-thieving bastard, playing at complacent and kind, a soft smile spreading across his face. And in his left hand, he held the exposed, gleaming blade of a straight razor.

I'm sure I fell completely pale, though of course it was impossible to tell. My reflection didn't become pale. Quite the opposite. He positively glowed. He raised the blade and flashed it in the light for me to see. Then he made this violent slashing motion through the air. Not surgical, not precise, just this insane, flurried slashing, cutting the space between us into a thousand little pieces. He let loose with what I assume was a maniacal laugh. I couldn't hear him through the mirror, but he looked positively giddy. Then he mouthed the words, "I'm going to kill you."

Old hat by now.

I scrambled out of the bathroom and slammed the door behind me. A few of my co-workers looked up from their desks, and I was too shaken to even try to play it off. I had to collect myself. I walked quickly, trying not to run, into the break room (there were no mirrors in there) and turned on the sink. I splashed my face with cold water and tried to clear my head. *I'm seeing things*, I thought. *I've gone all the way around the bend.* I rested my palms on the sink's edge and let the coolness of the metal spread up my arms. I took a few deep breaths and was about to turn back to the workroom when a sharp pain bit through my left hand. I screamed and jerked both hands from the polished metal of the sink. A line of bright red blood streaked against my palm. It dripped from my hand into the sink, right onto the face of my reflection, altered, warped, but still very visible in the smooth metal surface. He was waving the razor blade and laughing like a hyena.

I think this was about the time my brain decided to turn itself off.

I grabbed one of the break room towels (one of those ratty hand rags fraying at the edges and stained with years of coffee mop-ups) and tied it around the wound. The blood soaked all the way through almost instantly.

"Hey, you okay, guy?"

I whirled around, and there was Jim Johnson, from accounting, looking uncertain and twirling an empty mug on his finger. He'd come in for coffee and had found a crisis. I don't know why I remember this, but I distinctly noted that his eyes kept sliding over to the coffee pot, and I could practically hear him thinking, *Why today? Why me? I just wanted some goddamn coffee...*

Without a word (I don't think I could have mustered one if I'd tried), I shouldered past him and burst out of the break room. I stumbled down the hall and out of the office without an explanation to anyone. They'll probably fire me, I suppose, for just up and leaving like that, but honestly, who cares? I've got bigger problems.

He got me again in the elevator. I was in too much of a hurry. I wasn't thinking straight. I tumbled into the elevator and threw myself back against the far wall. As soon as my shoulders touched the polished metal, he flicked the razor. My jacket took most of the damage, but he nicked the skin just under the blade. I lunged forward, nearly slamming myself headfirst into the doors. He was standing there, too, ready. I caught myself just in time and teetered back into the center of the elevator. Thank God the floor was carpeted.

I made it to the lobby and ran out to my car. The underside of the door handle must be reflective metal, because as soon as I grabbed it, he sliced right into my fingers. Since I was pulling up on them when he struck, well... let's just say he did some damage there. Or let's just say I'm not likely to ever type again. Let's just say that.

I swatted the rearview mirror askew, spattering an arc of blood across the windshield. The woman getting out of the car next to me was probably like, *What the shit?* But what was I going to do, right? So I just started the car, backed out of the space, and drove 90 miles an hour until I was home.

Now what? Now what?

I paced through my living room, trying to decide on the best course of action, but let me tell you, it's not so easy to think straight when your reflection is slicing you to pieces. Holy shit, is that a distraction! It's safe to say (and is probably a huge understatement) that I was, and am, on the verge of a complete mental snap. The best thing to do, I decided, was to break the mirrors in the house. Give him no way to come through. I could have just taken them off the walls, I guess, but I wasn't about to take the chance of brushing up against the mirror surface when grabbing at the frames. Some of my mirrors don't even *have* frames. How was that going to work? And hell, by that point, I was ready for some catharsis. So I grabbed a baseball bat from the hall closet and went through the house, smashing every mirror I own.

Okay, yes, I know what you're thinking. "Didn't smashing your mirrors just make thousands of smaller mirrors, with a psychopathic murder reflected in each one?"

And the answer is... yeah. Yeah, it did.

Hindsight is 20/20. Shut up.

The next few minutes were... delicate. I'll just say, thank Christ I was wearing my shoes. They look more like pieces of a blown-out tire on the side of a freeway now, and my feet, well, yeah, they're bleeding, but it could've been worse. It could've been a lot worse.

So now, here I am, hiding away in my basement. It's the only place in the house with no mirrors, or mirror shards. It does have a few windows, though, and I can see him out of the corner of my eye. I see him beckoning me when the sunlight hits the panes just right. He desperately wants to kill me. And I can't think of a single place other than down here in the damp basement where I'd be entirely safe.

So here I sit. I haven't thought of a way out of this yet, but I'll come up with something. Right? *Something* will come to me. Something will come. I just have to—

Oh God. Who polished this floor?

In the Cards

Will sits quietly at the dining room table, thumbing at the lid of an old shoebox. They call it the dining room table, but that label is inexhaustive. It's also the kitchen table, the computer desk, the clean laundry hamper, a bill paying station, a writing desk, the parlor table, the beer pong board, and, every very memorable once in a while, a makeshift bed. But for the sake of brevity, it's been regulated to "the dining room table."

On any other day, there would be music playing, some new hipster band squawking from the cheap speaker dock in the living room (/guest room/yoga studio/study), their screeching guitars reverberating off every wall in the small Astoria apartment. Not today, though. Today, things are loud enough.

Angie's key clicks into the lock, and she barges through the front door, stamping her boots and laughing off the cold. "Oh! They turned on the heat!" she says, smiling and sighing and letting her wet coat slip off her shoulders. "Thank. God. This weather is my personal hell. Hi!"

"Hi."

"Our landlord is a sadist." She drops the coat into the corner and kicks her soggy boots on top of it. "If we had any self-respect, we'd set fire to his unit. But then ours would probably catch fire, and my shit would burn. Not like I have any good shit, but, you know. It's my shit. You know?"

"It's your shit," Will agrees. "How was work?"

"Ugh! Fantastic! I made more in tips tonight than the last three nights combined, and no one tried to grab my ass. It was all my dreams come true!"

"Good, good."

Angie rubs some warmth into her arms and steps in front of the large (but cracked) living room mirror, the one they'd salvaged from the sidewalk at Broadway and 46th on a trash day two years ago. She shakes out her hair, misting the mirror with little wet beads. "You know, everyone says blondes have more fun, but I don't know. I've been doing really well since going red. I think it makes me smolder." She purses her lips, trying to catch Will's eye in the reflection, but he's preoccupied with the shoebox.

"Mm," he says.

Angie bites the corner of her lip, a habit she's no longer aware of. "Oh, hey, remember when I sprained my ankle on the stairs a few weeks ago, that woman from downstairs who helped me? I saw her on my way out today, turns out a friend of her friend is casting a new show downtown, and she said she'd pass along my headshot! Isn't that fantastic?"

Will nods, once. "It's great. Yeah."

"She thinks she can get me an audition!"

"Great. That's really good."

Angie rolls her eyes and turns toward him. "All right. What's wrong?"

"Nothing."

"Will. What's wrong?"

"Do you know someone named Wallace Tab?" he asks, head low.

Angie starts. Will doesn't see it, but she does. "Wallace Tab? No, I don't think so. No. Yes. Wait. What, the writer?"

"I have no idea," Will says, shrugging. "Wallace Tab."

"I know a Wallace Tab. Or, I know of a Wallace Tab. He's a gossip columnist. Right? Or not?"

"Angie, I have no idea."

"Then why are you asking me if I know him?"

"You've never met him? In person?"

"Will. No. What's this about?" She makes the three steps from the living room mirror to the dining room table and plops down in the chair across from him. She leans back and plants her ankles on the table top. It is also a footrest.

"It's nothing." He stands up, picks up the shoebox, and walks toward the kitchen.

"What do you mean it's nothing? Why are you asking me that? Where are you going?"

"To the other room."

"What's wrong with this room?" Will doesn't answer, and now he's reached the kitchen (/linen closet/Pledge spray can storage space/toilet paper repository). "Will! Stop!"

He finally does, but he doesn't turn toward her. "What?"

"What is with you tonight?" Angie pulls her feet off the table top and stamps them on the faded wood floor.

"Nothing is with me."

"Something is obviously with you. Why did you ask if I know Wallace Tab?"

Will scoffs. He doesn't mean to, but he does. It's involuntary. "So you do know him."

Angie rolls her eyes again. "No! God, what is going on with you?"

"You're leaving me for him!" Will explodes. Well, there it is. He hadn't meant to say it out loud, at least not like that, but there it is. It hangs there.

Angie's hands spasm near her shoulders. Her classic disbelief posture. "What?"

"You're leaving me for him. For Wallace Tab."

Now she bursts out in laughter. She can't help it. The absurdity is too much. "That's insane! How am I supposed to leave you for someone I've never met?" she asks.

Will sighs. He tucks the shoebox under his arm and shuffles back into the dining room. "It's not insane." He returns to his chair, and Angie returns to hers. "Trust me."

"That's an outrageous thing to say. You know that, right?"

"I completely agree," he says. And he does. It's completely outrageous. But that doesn't make it any less true. He tells her so.

"Stop it! Why would you say that to me?" She tents her fingers against her chest, looking taken aback. Will isn't sure if it's a genuine reaction. He can rarely tell anymore. She really is a good actress. He hopes she gets that audition.

"If you don't know him yet, you're going to. It's right here." He reaches into his pocket and pulls out a three-by-five index card, the white kind with pale blue lines. He places it on the table and slides it over.

Angie raises one eyebrow (another classic Angie facial gesture) and picks up the card. "'She leaves you for Wallace Tab,'" she reads. Her eyebrow falls, and the look that follows seems a little more genuine. "What is this?"

Will sighs. "It's the future."

Angie laughs. Hysterical. "You are out of your mind! Did you type this?"

"No."

"Who did?"

"I don't know," he says.

"Where did you get it?"

"It came with the mail."

"Someone mailed this to you?"

Will shrugs. "I don't know if they mailed it. There's no postage. It was just in the mailbox, with the mail."

Angie flips the card over. It is blank on the back. "Wait. So hold on. This card showed up in our mailbox with no return address, no postage, makes a vague statement about "she" and "you," and it's the future? Are you serious?"

"Yes."

The laughter is throatier now, pushed up from a special, reserved place. "Oh, Will, you are out of your mind! It's a stupid prank, it's probably just Patrick, being an ass. You know Patrick's an ass. I know he's your best friend, but listen. He's an ass. Come on, have you eaten? I'm starving. I'll make pasta a la Ange." She tosses the card onto the table and heads toward the kitchen.

"It's not Patrick," Will says. To be honest, he's not 100% sure it's not Patrick, he's never asked. But he's pretty confident.

Angie shouts over her shoulder as she rummages through the pots under the sink. "Well, it looks like it was done on a typewriter. So it could be your grandmother. She's probably getting you back for that horrible scarf you gave her for Christmas last year. Remember that stupid thing? Oof. You're lucky she just sent a stupid card, I would have burned your house down."

Will appears in the doorway, index card in hand, shoebox under his arm. "Angie. Stop."

Angie finds the pot she's looking for, pulls it out, and drops it in the sink. She turns on the faucet. "Come on, Will. Someone's messing with you." But she doesn't turn to face him.

"It's not the only one."

"What's not the only what?"

"This note. It's not the only one."

Angie shuts off the water and puts the pot on the stove. She turns on the gas. It takes three tries to get the igniter to catch. "Well, what's the other one say?"

Will sets the card on the counter and pulls off the lid of the shoebox. It's disappointingly unceremonious. He's imagined this scenario so many times, and in his mind it's always been so dramatic. The Great Reveal. But now that he actually takes off the lid, it's not dramatic at all. It's clumsy. He can't help it, his hands are shaking. She's not even looking.

Angie opens the cabinet and pulls out a box of noodles. She tosses it onto the counter. Now she turns and sees the open box. It is filled with index cards. This time, her surprise is more natural. "These all came today?"

"No," Will signs, flipping through the cards. "They've been coming for years. They started showing up a few weeks after we met."

Angie stands, hands on hips, at a rare loss for words. She reaches out and snatches the shoebox from the counter and shuffles through the index cards. Each one is stamped with typewritten words. "What--what is this?"

"I don't know. I don't know where they come from, I don't know who writes them, I don't know anything about them except that they're all about you, and they're always right."

Angie looks up from the cards, and their eyes actually meet for what might be the first time since she came home (neither of them can remember for sure). "This isn't funny, Will."

"No, it's not."

"I'm serious! This isn't funny!"

"What, you think I'm having a ball of laughs over it?" He doesn't know what a ball of laughs is, he doesn't know why he said that. "I know it's not funny!"

"Why are you doing this?"

"Why am I doing what? I'm not doing anything!"

"You're screwing with me," she says, slamming the shoebox back down onto the counter. The water is starting to warm.

"I'm not."

"Well someone is!"

"Someone is," Will agrees. His arms are crossed so tightly that his left hand is going numb.

"What's that supposed to mean?" Angie snarls.

"When were you going to tell me about Wallace Tab?"

Angie explodes. She throws her hands into the air and leans into her scream. "There's nothing to tell! I don't even know him!"

"Bullshit!" Will roars. His voice sounds strange in his own ears. "That's bullshit!"

"Don't use that language with me!" she screams. Her eyes burn with anger and tears. "Don't you dare take that language with me! And don't call me a liar!"

"Then don't be a liar!" The water in the pot is starting to bubble. Tiny strings of oxygen pearls are streaming to the surface. Neither of them notices.

"I'm not! I don't know him!"

"Don't treat me like this!" Will screams. There's no other word for it. He doesn't yell, he doesn't holler, he doesn't shout. He screams. "Don't try to tell me this card is wrong, the cards are never wrong!" He grips a thick stack of the cards and pulls them out. He flips through them, reading each one, then throwing it to the floor and moving on to the next. "'She gets an audition for a play about Marie Curie,' 'She dyes her hair red,' 'She surprises you with Chinese take-out at work,' 'She gets cut from her show,' 'She forgets your birthday,' 'She gets promoted to head waitress.'" He throws the whole pile of cards onto the floor. They splay across the cheap tile. "347 cards, every single one of them came true within the week. So let's talk about number 348."

Angie's jaw won't unclench. It just won't. Because of this, when she speaks again, she's hissing. "Why didn't you tell me? Why didn't you tell me about this? Jesus, Will! Somebody knows my life?! Someone knows what's going to happen to me before it happens? Are you fucking kidding me? What is this? Why didn't you tell me?!"

"What am I supposed to say? 'Hey, Ange, some...what, some *person* out there knows your future and sends me an update every couple weeks, P.S., watch that first step, it's gonna be a doozy'? You'd think I was insane!"

"You knew." Angie's eyes narrow. They narrow so tightly that some part of Will wonders if she can still see through them. "You knew. Everything. This is my life, Will, and you--you knew everything!"

"I didn't know everything."

"You knew enough! Christ, Will! You knew I was getting cut from that show? You knew I was going to dye my hair, you knew I—" Suddenly, Angie has remembered something. "Oh my God." She attacks the shoebox of cards, rifling through them. They seem to be organized by date; it doesn't take her long to find the card she's looking for. She pulls it out, and she sinks to the floor. The pot has boiled over, and the flames are hissing against the water. "You knew."

Will doesn't ask which card she's holding. He doesn't need to. He knows. "Yeah," he says quietly. "I knew."

Her tears are awkward, and real. "Why didn't you say something?" she whispers.

"Ange…"

"Why didn't you say something?" she yells. Her voice is hoarse. "Why didn't you?"

She buries her face in her hands. It may be something she's been trained to do, it may be a new reaction. It may be real. "I panicked. I didn't know what to do, Will. I couldn't face it. I couldn't face you."

Will rubs the tears out of his own eyes. He reaches across the kitchen and turns off the stove. The flame goes out, the water stops hissing. He leans back against the wall and slides down it until he's joined her on the floor. "You should have told me," he says. He closes his eyes and plants his forehead against the heels of his hands. "She was mine, too."

Angie lifts her eyes. "It was a girl?"

Will just stares. "The cards aren't wrong."

Angie's hands fall limply to her sides. She has lost control over her body. It's a new experience. "If you knew, why didn't you--why didn't you leave?"

"Because I love you, Angie. Can you not see that? Because I want to be with you, unequivocally, always, you are--I couldn't lose you."

"And now?" she asks, her voice small.

"And now, I lose you anyway."

Angie nods slowly. The cards aren't wrong. "I leave you for Wallace Tab."

"Within the week."

She shakes her head. This is all so unreal. "It just doesn't make any sense," she says.

"Angie, tell me why." She keeps shaking her head, just keeps shaking her head. "Tell me why," he insists. "Tell me why I stood by you through this, through all of this, through everything. And the first time some other guy shows you how green his goddamn pasture is, you're out the door?"

"The first time? The first time? You have idea what I've given up for you, Will! What I've passed up for you! And don't tell me what you stood by, okay? I didn't know you knew, I didn't know you were 'standing by,' I thought I was alone in this, so don't you dare tell me you were 'standing by.' You have no idea what I go through."

"Actually, I do," he snarled, flicking one of the cards. It skitters across the floor and is lost under the stove. "Don't change the subject. I need to know why."

"Fine. You know why? Because you don't live! Nothing stimulates you anymore, Will! Nothing excites you, nothing about us excites you! It's like nothing between us even exists for you!"

Will laughs, once. He can't help it. He whispers, "Nothing surprises me."

This statement floats between them. It expands. It deflates.

"I didn't ask for this," he says, gesturing at the cards. "I don't want to know."

"I'm not the one doing it," she says. It's a weak defense.

Will wipes his eyes and slams his palms on the floor. "This can't be how it ends. Can it? It can't. The things I've done for you, the sacrifices I've made for you--for us. God, the knowledge about you that I've lived with, for years. All of it for you, and--and you just *leave*?"

Angie tucks her feet under her hips and leans forward, propping herself up on her forearms. A stretch she learned last month at the studio. "I'm not 'just' leaving. I've been agonizing over this. For a while. I hadn't decided on anything yet. But this...I mean, all this? You kept this from me. You knew so much. So much, Will! So many horrible things, and you didn't say anything? You knew things I'd do before I did them? Things that would happen to me? You could have done something! You could have stopped me from twisting my ankle or wrecking my car or adopting that stupid cat or having a goddamn abortion!" Something in her releases, and she is sobbing, her lungs are heaving, and she cannot breathe.

Will watches her lose control with interest. Something in him, something hidden, is satisfied by her tears. "Just because I knew doesn't mean they weren't your decisions," he says softly. "I can't live your life for you."

"Some life," Angie sobs.

"Some secrets."

Angie straightens up and scrubs at her eyes with her shirt. "I should go."

"You don't have to. We have a week."

"I should go now." She pushes herself off the floor and hurries into the bedroom, where she will find her overnight bag and pack enough clothes to hold her over for a few days. Will gets up and follows her in.

"What, so that's it?"

"What else is there?" she asks, throwing her sneakers into the bag.

"There's the future. The cards, Angie, if we know what's happening, we can change it. That's what you wanted, right? For me to act on them, stop your decisions? Fine! Let's do it! Stay! Stay here, and change them with me." This will work. He knows this will work. But she sniffles and shakes her head. "I can't. I can't. This is too much. I'm sorry." She stuffs the last piece of clothing into the bag and zips it closed. She hefts the bag onto her shoulder and pushes past him.

"You can!" he insists. "You don't have to go, we can make this work!"

Angie pauses at the front door, her hand on the knob. She lowers her head. She does not face him. "He comes into the restaurant," she says quietly.

"What?"

"Wallace Tab. He comes in. A lot. Has a thing for redheads, I guess. I know him, and we flirt, and we--I don't know. He was never--he's not the reason for this." She turns the knob, she opens the door, she slips out of the apartment, she is gone.

Over the next few days, the one pinpoint of solace in Will's inkwell of anger and confusion is that with Angie gone, the cards can stop coming, and at least, at the very, very least, this burden has been lifted. It is not enough, it is not nearly enough, but it is something.

But next week, there will be another card. It will say, "She throws away the album," and he will know that she's tossed out the pictures of the trip to Disney World they took three years ago. Two weeks later, he'll receive a card that says, "She skinny dips for the first time," and he'll become physically sick. Three weeks after that, he'll discover that she's in love. Ten more days, and he'll learn that they've gone to Paris together. In exactly four months, he'll find out that she's pregnant, and in four months and six days, he'll learn that she's keeping the baby.

The cards will never stop, and the cards will never be wrong.

Hugs or Drugs

Ah, Red Ribbon Week. That annual time of travesty when we encourage our students to say no to drugs while three-quarters of the faculty are taking the edge off next to the Dumpster behind the lounge. It's a time when we vow to keep kids off drugs, and to hell with us pesky adults; we had our chances during Red Ribbon Weeks 1987 through 1999. As part of this week of wonder, the students at this school are asked – nay, encouraged! – to wear red vinyl ribbons stamped with gilt lettering with any number of succinct phrases proclaiming the wearer's opposition to opiates. These phrases range from the admittedly unoriginal (dare I say unimpressive?) SAY NO TO DRUGS to the bold and astonishing (dare I say gripping?) TOBACCO IS WACKO! These embossed words herald the unquestionable drug-freeness of hundreds of students, including several dozen whom I would have sworn, prior to Red Ribbon Week, had most certainly shunned sobriety, but lo! In the face of such irrefutable red-vinyl proof, I am forced to admit my error! If that bloodshot, shambling hippie in second period is wearing a SAY NOPE TO DOPE badge of pride, he is proudly proffering his personal purity, and aren't I the fool for doubting his chemical abstinence! For as we all know, so it is stamped on a red vinyl ribbon, so shall it be!

Don't mistake me: I have great respect and admiration for the Red Ribbon drug-awareness program. But seriously, the awareness of drugs isn't just half the battle against them, it's also three-fifths of the case *for* them. "Crystal meth, you say? I've never heard of that! Please, I'm an inquisitive youth, won't you tell me more about it?" Oh, it's a precarious line those Red Ribboners walk, so carefully acknowledging the existence of drugs without encouraging further investigation by experimentation. Clever is the soul who first decided to elevate the conversation by channeling it through a series of golden quips on slippery swaths of scarlet, for in my experience, there is nothing high schoolers enjoy more than wholesome, non-ironic misdirection.

But despite my wholehearted enthusiasm for this groundbreaking and eminently successful campaign, I must admit, there is one ribbon slogan in particular that gives me pause. I feel that this idiom, while blessedly and admirably succinct, ultimately limits the wearer as a cognizant chooser. The slogan to which I refer, of course, is HUGS, NOT DRUGS.

HUGS, NOT DRUGS. What a seemingly innocuous turn of phrase! In a sense, its simplicity is nothing short of elegant. In a space of three words, all literate passersby are informed that drugs are bad, and that hugs are a far more preferable option. Many cite this particular slogan as a favorite, but personally, I find two significant issues contained therein:

First of all, how many times has a potential drug purchaser been faced with the implied choice?

"Hey, kid. You wanna buy some drugs?"

"Yes, please."

"You got money?"

"Tons!"

"You ain't a cop, are you?"

"No, sir."

"And you're sure you wouldn't rather buy some hugs?"

"No, I—waaaaaaaaait a minute. Hugs?"

"Yeah, hugs. You lookin' to score hugs or drugs?"

"Well, I initially thought drugs, but *now…*"

"Hurry up, kid, I got people to see."

"Don't rush me, I'm thinking! Hugs or drugs... hmmm... hugs... or... drugs..."

That doesn't happen. That has *never* happened. Not even in the movies, where all the things that have never happened have happened. The idea is preposterous. In my experience, people looking to buy drugs are wholly unconcerned with hugs (though, admittedly, the same might not be true for those lonely hearts doing the selling). And even if drug addicts did decide they wanted hugs instead of drugs (or even in addition to drugs), they wouldn't give their hard-earned drug money to purchase them. Hugs are basically free. It's ludicrous.

My second problem with the HUGS, NOT DRUGS slogan is that though I certainly don't condone drugs, I also don't condone genial physical closeness. There are about three people in the entire universe I would even let close enough to be able to hug me. Everyone else in the world can just go right to hell. And as for actually hugging those jokers? Forget it. I ain't hugging jack. ("Jack" as in "nothing," not "jack" as in a person named Jack, though it works both ways; if I knew a Jack, I wouldn't hug him.)

I hate hugging people. It makes me uncomfortable. If you're close enough to dampen me with your sweat, you're way too close. If I want to be covered in sweat that badly, I'll make my own sweat, and if I'm so damn keen to do that, I'd just as soon do drugs in the first place. Those meth addicts are like walking glasses of lemonade. Sweat, sweat, sweat. So what the hell kind of option is this? Hugs or drugs? If I choose the one, I become an addle-brained shell of a man bent on self-destruction, and if I choose the other, I become addicted to drugs. *Boom!* But seriously, hugs or drugs? That's not a choice. That's some bullshit. Hell, I'd probably take drugs over hugs from 97% of the people I know. At least drugs can make you feel good for a while.

Okay, but no, I don't condone drug usage. It's bad, all right? It's bad. But neither do I condone hugs. And seriously, if the Red

Ribbon students think they're going to solve the nation's drug problems with PDA, I've got news for them. It's called the Student Handbook. Look it up. Even if students *were* allowed to touch each other on school property, you really think hugs would solve anything? *EHHHNN!* Wrong. We're not dealing with four-year-old pansy-ass children here. We're dealing with crack addicts who soil their own pants. And if you want to hug that, knock yourself out.

Ah, hell, there's the bell. Just think about what I said, all right? Seriously. And let's all just be grateful that gin's not a drug, because I swear to god, third period's impossible without it.

Cold Feet

Holding the ceremony at the Church of the Power of Suggestion wasn't Manny's idea. Of course, very few aspects of the wedding were. Except for the marriage itself. That was one point upon which they most certainly agreed, and it was all he really cared about when it came right down to it. So he had happily left the details of the wedding to Claudia, his dulcet bride-to-be (who – let's be honest – would have demanded them anyway, by force if necessary, had he not given them over willingly). Claudia had chosen the floral arrangements (daises and ivy), the color scheme (chocolate brown and emerald green), the seating arrangements for the reception (keep Mom away from the cake table), and a thousand other details that would, she was sure, cap the perfect wedding, including the selection of the church. Manny had never heard of the Church of the Power of Suggestion, nor had he any modicum of an idea as to what religion might claim it. Methodists, maybe? He had always been a little wary of Methodists. That was probably it.

At any rate, he now found himself standing proudly at the back of the church, hands clasped smartly over his dapper black-and-chocolate-brown tuxedo as the wedding planner who demanded to be referred to as "the Jaquelle" deftly pinned an emerald green boutonnière to his lapel. "Cold feet," she murmured in her foreign gypsy voice.

"Pardon?" asked Manny, who had been entirely too busy being

happy to pick up on her guttural utterings.

"Cold feet," she replied, in the exact same tone. "You got cold feet."

Manny smirked an amused little smirk. "Not me," he said confidently. "I've been waiting for this day my whole life."

"Is vat zey all say," answered the Jaquelle with a shrug. "But don't vorry. You get zem."

"Ha, ha! Never!" replied poor Manny. For how was he to know? And as the orchestra swelled, the Jaquelle gave his cheek a pinch for good luck, spun him around, and pushed him down the aisle.

It was a much longer walk than he would have guessed. The aisle seemed to stretch and stretch before him, like a hallway in a horror film. And as he walked, he had plenty of time to think. What if he *did* get cold feet? What would happen then? Would he know he'd gotten cold feet? What were the telltale signs? And, heavens, more importantly, what if Claudia had cold feet? Or was it called something else for the bride? Womanly whim, he thought he read somewhere. No, he decided. Claudia was too fiercely determined to see this through to a fairytale ending, even if she had to murder a bridesmaid in cold blood to achieve it. (This wasn't conjecture; she'd said as much.) Claudia wouldn't have a womanly whim. But what if *he* had a womanly whim? Er, cold feet? How would he know? And could he handle it?

All these thoughts and more batted about inside Manny's thick head as he ambled his way to the front of the church. He took his position on the first step, just as they had practiced the night before, and waited, for the first time with some nervousness, for the wedding to begin. And as he waited for the procession of groomsmen and bridesmaids to march down the aisle, something strange happened. Something very strange indeed. Manny got cold feet. Not metaphorically, but *literally*. His feet grew very cold.

This surprised Manny greatly, because he had mistakenly put on wool socks that morning instead of his cotton ones, something he'd been sure he would live to regret. But as he stood there, his toes became very numb, as if they were bare and planted in a mound of snow. Then his heels began to tingle, and an icy grip took hold of both soles. Manny's mind careened between his ears. How could this be happening? It was June, for crying out loud! And yes, sure, the air conditioning was on in the church, but it wasn't *that* strong. He wriggled his toes as best he could, which was not very much, and wondered with no small amount of awe if "getting cold feet" *actually* meant getting cold feet!

Poor, poor Manny.

He wondered, then, if he felt any unease about the ceremony now that he had cold feet. He checked, and double-checked, and triple-checked, and he searched his feelings, and he found that he still had absolutely no doubts whatsoever about the marriage. Had he triumphed over the cold feet, then?

The procession began. The best man, a good friend of Manny's by the name of Maxwell Tooth, escorted the lovely (but desperately pimple-ridden) maid of honor, Lyla Cant. Manny smiled at them as they approached the altar, and they at him. But as they approached, his smile faltered, because he noticed something else quite strange. The chill seemed to be moving up his legs! He could feel it in his calves, a bitter stiffness that locked in his knees and did not allow him to move. This was most troubling, for several reasons. First of all, his legs were turning to ice with no readily available explanation, and this is always a cause for concern. Second, if he were not able to walk or kneel (and he was certainly not, now that the ice had crept up to thigh level—heavens, thigh level!), how would he possibly go through with the ceremony?

Panic spread throughout his body, and, under normal circumstances, a sweat would have broken out across his brow. As it stood, however, he was too chilled to sweat, which, on the whole, was probably a good thing. This was a better look for the camera.

The procession continued, with groomsmen lagging always half a step behind the bouncing, beaming (but secretly begrudging) bridesmaids. The air was electric with the energy of a marriage to be, but Manny noticed none of it – not a single shock of it – because by the time the last groomsman had settled in his place to Manny's left, the ice had reached his chest, and he was finding it hard to breathe. There he stood: cold, numb, frozen from toe to sternum, unable to respire, unable to signify what was wrong, because oh, how would he even begin, had he the breath to speak? Poor, miserable Manny!

And the ice continued to spread. The fanfare announcing the arrival of his bride began, the guests stood, the doors were thrown open, and there, in the doorway, surrounded by a perfectly timed halo of sunlight, stood the most radiant bride in the history of the Church of the Power of Suggestion, one who was positively alight with joy and prospective bliss! But Manny, dear Manny, he barely gave her a second glance! His arms were becoming cold now, deathly cold, and then his hands; oh, his hands! As the feeling spread finally to the exposed skin of his wrists, he saw with absolute certainty that his hands (and, he assumed, his entire besuited body) had turned an icy shade of blue! And what's more, they were filmed over by a crust of real, honest-to-goodness ice! Manny looked around wildly, as far to the right and left as his frozen body would allow. Was no one else seeing this? But they were all, every one of them, gazing breathlessly at Claudia, the gorgeous bride, as she goose-stepped her way toward the altar.

And here he was, freezing to death! In the middle of June! What had started as cold feet was now cold *everything*! Everything, save his head. But it wouldn't be long now, would it? No, it wouldn't be long now, not long at all! And as his bride ascended to join him on the first step, Manny's face glazed over with a sheet of sleek blue ice, and it covered his mouth, his nose – good heavens, his eyes! – up, up, up, turning his hair into frozen, well-gelled stalagmites, and Manny was – there was no doubt – completely, entirely, utterly frozen! He was naught but a solid block of man-shaped ice!

And Claudia, dear Claudia, who had been positively blinded by the incessant camera flash bulbs popping around her as she walked down the aisle, saw not the blue complexion nor the look of fear and terror that was, very literally, frozen onto her fiancé's face. And she took his hand, his icy blue hand, as she had been instructed to do at the rehearsal, and when she felt its wet, chilling cold, she yelped with surprise, and she jumped in surprise, too, and oh, horror of horrors! She jumped right into poor Manny, who, unable to control his frozen muscles, tottered back and forth on his blasted cold feet and, with nothing to keep him aright, fell right over onto the floor with a mighty crash, shattering into a zillion little Manny pieces, simultaneously ruining both the rented tuxedo and the wedding, as well as, it can be assumed, the life of the was-once-to-have-been bride!

Believe me when I tell you, darling, that this is a true story. I swear my life on it. And now you see, of course, the perils of staging a wedding and, more importantly, why I cannot possibly marry you today, or ever. I do hope you understand.

Sorry for the late notice.

Warmly yours,

Benson Prig

The Amazing Brutillo

Clare had never been to the circus before, nor had she really ever had the desire. A traveling show was a common thing, a farcical spectacle better beheld by twelve-year-old boys with romantic notions of wonder than by a woman in her late twenties who had begun to abandon the idea of romance altogether. But Robert had insisted, always the twelve-year-old boy at heart (often to his detriment), and he was rather appalled at the fact that she had managed to remain ignorant of the "magic of the big top," as he put it, for so many years. Now, sitting beneath the ratty, faded, red and white tent, she was certain that it was an experience she could have done without. Most of the tent was crowded with screaming, ogling children, and the animals on display were worn, pathetic creatures with tired eyes. It pulled at her heart to see them cajoled around the makeshift dirt ring at the center of the floor. But her fiancé seemed to be enjoying himself immensely, and she did her best to mimic his enthusiasm.

After an hour of lion tamers, juggling clowns, and an admittedly interesting tightrope walking exhibition that almost ended in a coroner's investigation, the lights dimmed to an ominous dusk, and a spotlight flooded the center ring. The ringmaster, a pudgy Italian man in a tight-fitting red tuxedo jacket with a torn seam at the left shoulder, stepped into the spot and called for attention as he presented the main attraction of the night, a man whose mysterious powers, he claimed, had been honed by the most powerful and terrifying witch doctors of the Dark Continent, a man for whom the very breath of the earth was at the slightest command, the one, the only, the Amazing Brutillo!

Clare exploded with laughter at the ridiculousness of the name. Robert threw her a pleading look, and she covered her mouth with her hand, blushing bright red as the spectators around her grumbled at her rudeness. She couldn't help it, though. The Amazing Brutillo? It sounded more like a cleaning solution than a man.

The spotlight cut out, and a thick blue mist rolled into the tent. It piled upon itself, becoming taller and thicker, gathering into spinning clouds. The fog slowly began to take shape, and the shape settled into itself, lost its translucence, and when the spotlight cut back to the center, the mist had formed into a man. There before the awed crowd stood the great magician, the Amazing Brutillo!

Even Clare had to admit it was an impressive entrance.

Brutillo was not much for small talk. He set straight to work, motioning to the edge of the ring, where two clowns wheeled a large crate onto the dirt floor. The box, about six and a half feet tall and three feet wide, had the look of a coffin standing on end, except for the fact that it was painted in dark, luscious red with a gaudy, golden trim. The clowns rolled the crate to the center of the ring, next to its owner, and then skittered out of the dirt ring, kicking at each other and scuffing plumes of dust into the air. Children laughed nervously, and Clare found herself absently squeezing Robert's hand. Brutillo's steady, stony gaze and thin-lipped grimace held such a contrast to the circus merriment that, well...the effect was unsettling.

He set into motion a fluid routine, first spinning the box in a circle so all could see it from every angle, then opening the front panel, then the rear panel, then spinning it again so the audience could see straight through the crate, then stepping into the half opened box and stamping on its base to prove its sturdiness and to dispel any ideas of trap doors. Finally satisfied, he stepped out of the box with a very slight flourish, closed both panel doors, and gave it one final spin.

Some of the children craned their necks in anticipation. Others yawned, bored with the lack of color and music. Most of the adults caught themselves raising eyebrows at each other. What wonder was about to unfold? Finally, Brutillo spoke.

"Ladies and gentlemen," he said in a velvety baritone, "I would ask for a volunteer."

Was it Clare's imagination, or was he staring directly at her?

Perhaps egged on by the direction of the magician's glance, perhaps simply out of excitement, Robert nudged her with his elbow. "Raise your hand," he whispered out of the side of his mouth. Clare let out a quick guffaw. "You can't be serious." "Come on, it'll be a gas!" And he grabbed her hand and hoisted it in the air. "Robert!" She wrenched her wrist from his grasp and pulled it down, but it was too late. The Amazing Brutillo had selected his prey.

"You, miss," he said, holding up a hand in Clare's very specific direction. "In the red blouse." Heavy groans from unchosen children fell like cold lead around the tent, but they were completely outdone by Robert's laughter.

"Welcome to the circus," he beamed.

Clare briefly considered breaking the engagement.

One of the spotlights had picked her up now, and she shielded her eyes against the glare. "Nowhere to run," said Robert, rather stupidly, she thought. "Good luck!" Now the crowd was applauding. Brutillo waited patiently at the bottom of the risers, hand outstretched. A second spotlight caught her in its beam. She really did have nowhere to go but down. With a bit of pointed grace, she goose-stepped her way to the aisle and walked down to meet the magician's hand. He did not smile as he beheld her, and his apparent coldness worried her more than a little.

"What is your name, my dear?" he asked evenly as he led her to the crate.

"Clare," she said, a little too harshly. She didn't want to look as apprehensive as she felt.

"Clare, have we ever met before?"

"No." Up close, his features were much sharper, much darker. His eyes were coal black and burned at the edges with a dark orange flame. If they had met before, she would have remembered, with eyes like that…

The magician opened the front panel of the cabinet and ushered her inside. She bit her bottom lip and looked up into the stands for Robert, but the spots were too harsh, and she could see nought but a wall of white light. She shielded her eyes, and there he was, beaming and nodding, overjoyed that her first circus experience was turning out to be so unique. "Idiot," she muttered, and she stepped into the empty box.

"Inspect the floor, please. Make sure there is no trap door," said her captor. She stomped on the floor, and it did indeed appear to be quite solid. He spun the crate, slowly and carefully, so everyone could see Clare standing uncomfortably inside. "Ladies and gentlemen," he addressed the crowd, "what you are about to witness is no mere parlor trick. What you are about to experience…is magic." With a flourish, he spun back to the box and started to haul the panel closed.

"Wait!" whispered Clare. "What do I do?"

"You disappear," Brutillo said quietly, almost sadly. Clare wished he would smile. And then, as he swung the door shut and latched it in place, it suddenly dawned on her what was so unsettling about his expression. It wasn't mean or cruel, or even uncaring. It was worried.

And then the darkness of the box enveloped her, and something down below was scraping at her leg.

Having latched the box closed, the Amazing Brutillo motioned to the clowns to come forward. They did, holding a large purple throw between them, which they draped over the box. It fit perfectly over the frame, the tips of the sheet just brushing against the dirt floor. The clowns were excused. The magician circled the box, running his fingers along the drape and muttering a spell too low for the audience to hear. And then, without preamble, Brutillo whisked away the purple covering, and the box beneath buckled and opened, the four walls and the top fell away on hinges, and the entire thing collapsed, flat and exposed, onto the dirt floor. Clare was nowhere to be seen.

The crowd erupted in violent applause. Robert cheered louder than anyone. This would certainly give her a story to tell when they went to visit his family next week! He silently hoped she was paying close attention to the trick, wherever she was, and could perhaps shed light on its secret after they left the show. Magic had always interested him, and he was a man who yearned to know secrets.

Brutillo rolled the box away from its current position to show that there was no trap door in the dirt floor of the arena and that there was surely not enough space between the bottom of the box and the ground for a person to escape. When the applause died down, he circled the felled box, hoisting the sides and returning them to their upright positions. When the box was whole once again, he gave it a sharp spin. After one full revolution, he caught one of the corners with one hand, stopped the spinning, and pulled open the panel.

The box was still empty.

Robert was jerked from his musings by a sharp drop in his stomach. The box was empty? Why was the box empty? Shouldn't Clare be back inside now? Wasn't that the point of the trick? The flourish? The prestige, or whatever they called it? Where was she?

He laughed to himself. There's more to the trick, he thought. Of course. But something about the magician's expression was wrong. He seemed...sad.

"Brutillo!" shouted Robert, jumping up from his seat and making for the aisle. "Brutillo!" A general panic was welling up within the tent. It was frightfully clear to everyone that Clare should have been safely returned. Robert rushed down to the dirt floor, his heart slamming against his chest. He locked eyes with the sorrowful magician, sky blue meeting coal black. And then, before Robert could reach him, the illusionist did something rather unsettling.

He disappeared in a puff of smoke.

The police investigation turned up very little. Clare had not been found. The Amazing Brutillo, for his part, had simply vanished. Disappeared without a trace, his personal trailer still cluttered with his clothes, his trunk stored safely in the closet, his personal effects still littered around the room...but no magician to claim them. He was simply gone. The circus had no forwarding address, no contact information whatsoever. The company hadn't even documented his real name. It just wasn't something that was done in the trade, the ringmaster explained. Every officer in the small town sheriff's office spent the next 12 hours trying to track down Brutillo, and while they were distracted, the circus packed itself up in the middle of the night, and it, too, vanished completely by dawn.

The next day, it was as if the circus had never come to town.

Robert spent the next week in a perpetual state of shock. Clare was gone. She was really, truly, impossibly, but incredibly gone. A harmless magic trick, a sleight of hand, a misdirection by a vagrant conjurer, and his fiancée had become a photo on the missing persons board. The sheriff's bumblers couldn't even agree on where to *begin* the investigation. The man responsible had disappeared as completely as the victim, and there were absolutely no telling clues left at the scene of the crime. If it was a crime. That's what one of the policemen had said. *If it was a crime.* Robert had exploded. Of course it was a crime! It was kidnapping, it was bodily harm, it was probably murder! How could it not be a crime? But the detectives were as clueless as anyone else.

Weeks passed, then months, and although the investigation was never officially called off, it was eventually abandoned. What else was there to do? The entire town had been searched, then the neighboring towns, then the whole county. Bulletins had been posted, first across the state, then across the country. Her picture had been sent to the bureaus of all major cities. A reward was offered. Reports had flooded the airwaves. Still, not so much as a single lead surfaced. Clare was gone. Clare was gone. The police gave up hope. By the next summer, her family seemed ready to give up, too. After two years, Robert knew he must resign himself to the fact that she was dead.

Clare, his Clare, was dead.

A decade passed. Clare was never forgotten, but her family, citing too many memories, had moved out of town not long after her disappearance. Robert remained, despite the fact that it was not his hometown. He had moved there to be with Clare. But now that she was gone, it didn't seem right for him to leave. It would have been abandonment. She wouldn't have wanted that. And so life continued for Robert, sort of, and friends eventually stopped feeling abashed around him, and he eventually mustered up the courage to give away her things, and sleep eventually returned to his house. Most nights, anyway. Sometimes, he would find himself standing on his balcony in the pre-dawn hours, staring blindly into the night, both seeing and not seeing the trees whitewashed in the ghostly pallor of the moon. Clare had loved walking through the grove in the nighttime, and it was sleepless nights like these that he missed her the most. It was fitting, then, that it was just such a bright, pale night when he saw her, clawing her way through the grove, struggling through the grass, up the hill to the house, caked in grime and blood.

At first he thought it was an animal, a dog, maybe, or an injured wolf. But as the figure staggered into the moonlight, he saw her knotted black hair and her shredded red blouse, saw her bleeding legs, her bone white knuckles digging at the earth, heard her very human moans of pain, and he knew it was her, it was Clare, the ghost of Clare, come to haunt him.

Hot tears stung his eyes as he flew down the stairs and threw open the back door of the house. They blurred his vision as he ran down the hill, and he tripped over some unseen divot, went sprawling into the grass, clamored back to his feet, ran again. He came upon her and skidded to a stop in the wet grass.

It wasn't a ghost. It was *her*. It was really, truly, impossibly her! She was battered, and bloodied, and bruised, and broken. Her clothes were torn, her hair mangled, one eye swollen shut, one leg twisted out at a sickening angle, but it was her. It was his Clare.

Dr. Baker repacked his medical bag and snapped it shut. "She's in bad shape," he admitted. "She's in real bad shape. But give it enough time, and she'll heal." He stuck a second pillow under her set leg. "Physically, at least." He said this last quietly, almost to himself, as he brushed a few loose strands of hair away from Clare's bruised cheek. Her eyes were open, and she was awake, technically, though she showed no other signs of it. Dr. Baker stood from the bed and motioned silently for Robert to follow. Once in the hall, he closed the door to the bedroom behind them and turned with pity. "There's no telling what all she's been through," he said, slowly shaking his head. "There's just no telling. Whatever it was, must've been awful bad. She's drawn up inside herself tighter than Ebenezer's purse strings."

"Will she come out of it?" Robert asked hoarsely.

"No telling," said the doctor, shaking his head. "There's just no telling."

Robert loaded his pistol and spun the chamber, a nervous habit he had developed of late. He blinked his heavy lids, trying to force the world back into focus. He was weary, physically and mentally, but his journey was nearing its end.

Three months had passed since Clare's return, and for all he knew, she was still catatonic. By the time he had left, one week after her reappearance, she hadn't so much as blinked, despite his panicked efforts to coax her free of the invisible grip that held her. Now it was time for answers. He had to know what happened to her. He had to understand. If he knew where she'd been, he could find a way to bring her back to herself, he knew he could. But that wasn't all. Something deep within him itched to understand her plight, to see for himself what could have possibly terrified her to the point of detachment from reality. He had to see what she saw. And so he had left her in the hands of Miss Havish, his widowed neighbor, who would stay with Clare in the house and notify the family by wire if her condition changed.

He had spent the last few months traveling around the country, visiting every traveling circus he could track down. The particular company responsible for Clare's disappearance was long gone, of course. In name, at least. But the show itself still traveled under a different name, under different colors, he was certain of that. Circus freaks know only one life.

His journey had brought him through seven states, to over three dozen wandering carnivals. Each failure grated on his spirit, but they also brought him one step closer to his prey. Now, at last, he had succeeded, had found the circus, finishing up a tour of small towns in eastern Indiana. He recognized the ringmaster, with his cheap red tuxedo jacket, torn at the seam in the left shoulder. The same coat, after all these years. The same coat. The same man.

Now he stood in the fat Italian's trailer, the ringmaster himself bound securely to a chair by thick tent rope. Sweat poured down his great, meaty brow, plastering his thin mustache to his pudgy cheeks. He bawled like a coward.

"You have to let me go! You don't know what you're doing! Please, this is--this is senseless, if I remembered, I'd tell you, but--"

"You remember," said Robert. He spun the chamber in the gun again and hefted the weapon. "Of course you remember. Had to change your name and run away because of it, didn't you? Can't forget a little thing like that." He walked up to the sobbing ringmaster and knelt before him, pressing the barrel of the gun against the ankle of his right foot. "I just want a name."

The man palsied in the chair. "I told you, I don't know his name!" he shrieked. "He just came on as Brutillo, I don't know his real name! I never--" The bullet exploded through his ankle, shattering the bone and splattering gore against the flimsy trailer wall. The Italian screamed until he was hoarse.

It was going to be a long night.

Santano was wary of any visitors, but especially so at this time of night. He had pushed aside the curtain and peered out into the darkness, and even with the moon hidden by the midnight storm clouds, he had recognized the face. It was a face from a different time, when Santano had used a different name. Which one, who could remember? But across the deep chasm of years, he had known the face.

Now the two men stood in Santano's shed, where he kept his magical tools, though he hadn't worked them in ages. It was dangerous keeping all these props, he knew, but some things he couldn't bring himself to part with, and others were too powerful to be set free.

They stood before the red and gold box, the portal that had changed the course of the young man's life all those years ago. Robert held a gun at Santano's stomach, his eyes red-rimmed with exhaustion, or insanity, or both. There was dry blood caked on his hands, almost certainly not his own. He looked as if he hadn't slept or bathed in weeks. And now, here he was, demanding answers.

"That was the first night I used it," Santano said quietly. "I had tested it, of course, but not with an actual person. With puppets, if I recall accurately. There was a man in the show, his name was... Reibus? Raimus? He carved such beautiful figures. It was an obsession for him, truly. He was quite literally drowning in wooden puppets, so he let me use them for my trial runs. But I always saved the real test for the opening night audience, you see. With this trick or any other, I never used a real person until show time. Cheap thrills, I suppose." He scoffed quietly. "Foolish. But it had worked with the puppets, brought them back, and they, of course, were sedentary. How could it go differently with an animate object, with a person who could reason, who could think her way out of a box with the most perfunctory mental processes? There was no reason, absolutely no reason, to believe it wouldn't work as well with a living person." It looked so unassuming, the box, standing there in the dim light, covered in dust.

"How does it work?" Robert rasped. "How is it *supposed* to work?"

"I don't know."

"How can you not know? Didn't you build it?"

"No, of course not. I never had the skill for carpentry. I purchased it from a man by the name of Lewis Callweather. I purchased all my magical trinkets through him. I trusted him."

"You bought it without knowing how it works?" Robert laughed shrilly. The sound fell dead against the worn oak beams of the shed. "I'm supposed to believe that?"

"What you do or do not believe it of little concern to me. I tell you only what happened. He said I had to figure it out for myself, it was like always. He demonstrated the effect and gave me the simplest instructions on how to achieve it, but it was for me to learn the true secret. It was a game we played. It was a game that, until this box, I had mastered, but this...this was a mystery to me. Callweather had certainly outdone himself. In fact, I intended to keep your fiancée after the show to ask her about the experience, help me learn how the trick worked. But, as you know, I never got the chance."

Robert remembered how, so long ago, he, too, had been so looking forward to discussing the particulars of the trick with Clare. The memory brought fresh tears to his eyes, and he scrubbed them away angrily with his mottled sleeve. "You've ruined our lives," he hissed.

Santano gazed back at him with black, baleful eyes. "Yes," he said. "I know."

Robert looked up at the dusty crate. "I want to know," he whispered. "I need to know where she went."

"Yes," Santano said again, turning his own gaze to the box as well. "I suppose you do."

Robert stepped into the chamber. Under other circumstances, he imagined he would have felt skittish, nervous, even terrified. But standing there in the dusty crate, he felt nought but detaching numbness. There was really nothing else left to do. He had to know. He had to know. For his sweet Clare's sake, and for his own gnawing itch. He had to know.

Santano held the panel door open and raised a hesitant eyebrow. "Are you sure you want to do this?" Robert nodded. Santano grimaced, nodded sadly, and latched the door shut. A quick spin on creaking casters, a trace of the fingers through the dust, and when he opened the box, Robert was gone.

Santano was uncomfortable with lies. A strange moral for such a man to latch on to, yes, but there it was. He'd much prefer to tell the truth whenever possible, but it rarely was. If he told the truth, they'd never step into the box. He stroked the gilded edges tenderly, tracing meaningless runes in the dust. He needed them to step inside. He needed to send them down.

In time, he would let Robert out. The creatures below would need a change in their diet. Well, he supposed need was an indulgent word. A change wasn't strictly *necessary*, the dark magic of the box saw to that. The victim's constant flesh regeneration meant the creatures could feed for all of eternity. But there were so many flavors to behold, and he was such a doting father. He wanted so much for his children.

The Amazing Santano left the shed and padlocked the door. Next week, perhaps, he would begin searching out a new circus.

He felt invigorated, ready to resume his work. And it was time for a new name. Clinging to any one moniker for an extended period left him feeling…clammy. Ah, but he'd work that out in the morning. The name he signed to any given company was ultimately unimportant.

It was the act that mattered, and the act was always the same.

The Castle Dim

Sir Bimmiden stood with his chin propped up on the stone windowsill of Castle Dim and gazed forlornly out at the dry swath of land below. The stone was cold against his chin, which had started to go numb, but he felt this dramatic pose was absolutely necessary to really get his point across. To accentuate things, he sighed heavily. For perhaps the seventeenth time. His companion, however, remained (or pretended to remain, perhaps) hopelessly oblivious, lost in his one-man game of chess, which he was, incidentally, losing. Bimmiden had been trying oh-so-subtly to get his attention for at least seven minutes now. It was time for stronger action.

"Sir Fiddius," began Bimmiden, still visually pondering the small bit of kingdom entrusted to the two of them. "Sir Fiddius, when do you think we shall be attacked?"

"Pardon?" asked Fiddius, who was not hard of hearing, but often pretended he was in order to bypass conversations such as these.

"I said, when do you think we shall be attacked?" Bimmiden repeated. The deaf ploy was clearly not going to work this time. With a great sigh of his own, Fiddius tried, unsuccessfully, to end the game by capturing his own knight, and instead somehow found his king's bishop in checkmate, a move that deeply disturbed him.

He did not understand how to play chess.

"Why do you think we are to be attacked?" he asked, rather

blandly. Bimmiden peeled his jaw from the cold stone sill and began to pace furiously along the cold stone floor. "Wew in a cathle," he began, his frozen jaw not working properly now that it wasn't propped up by the sill. He vigorously rubbed life back into it and began again. "We're in a castle, right?" Fiddius nodded his agreement. "And castles get attacked, right?" Fiddius pondered this one for a few seconds.

"Some of them do, yes," he admitted, "but... but I think—" He was on the cusp of putting a full idea together. "I think... maybe some castles don't," he finished confidently.

"Preposterous!" cried Bimmiden. "I've never known a castle not to be attacked! All castles must be attacked!"

"What about Camelot?" Fiddius dutifully pointed out. "No one's attacked Arthur's castle yet."

"Well, of course no one's attacked *Arthur's* castle yet!" Bimmiden found himself getting quite worked up. "No one would dare attack *Arthur's* castle, would they? I didn't mean *his* castle!"

"You said all castles."

"Oh, shut up. All regular castles not guarded by a great wizard, a wise king, and an enchanted sword, then. All regular castles not guarded by a great wizard, a wise king, and an enchanted sword must be attacked!" Fiddius had to concede that this might be a true statement. "Now," continued Bimmiden, resuming his frantic pacing, "as you well know, we have not been attacked. I demand to know why. I demand that we be attacked!"

The strangeness of this statement did not go unnoticed by Fiddius. "Well... maybe it's better if we're not attacked, Sir Bimmiden."

"What?! Preposterous! How can that possibly be better than being attacked?"

"Well," said Fiddius slowly, as he chewed over the words crashing out of his mouth, "when castles get attacked, they get attacked by full armies. Right?'

"Obviously!" Bimmiden's pacing had now morphed into a full-out circle of impatience.

"And then... when a castle is attacked, it is defended with that castle's army, right?"

"Yes, of course. What's your point?"

"My point is..." He stopped and did a mental check as to the validity of what he was about to say. It seemed to pass the test. "My point is... we ain't got no army. There's only two of us. I think we'd lose."

"Impossible! We are knights of Camelot! Dispatched by Arthur himself to govern and protect this province! And the knights of Camelot do not lose!"

"Well, Gawain took a pretty bad beating last month..."

Bimmiden ignored this and pressed on. "Besides, there are more than two of us, you dolt. We've got the entire cooking staff, and that makes five."

"I don't think they're trained in combat, Sir Bimmiden."

"Oh, it doesn't matter! It's the presence that matters! Five people is a lot more intimidating than two people, isn't it?" Fiddius admitted that it was. "Besides! This is a heavily fortified castle! An opposing army would surely crash and fall against its iron walls of stone!" To accentuate his point, Bimmiden pounded a fist against the common room wall. A piece of it crumbled and fell to the floor.

"Unless, of course, they got in the castle," concluded Fiddius. "Then I should say we'd have a bit more trouble."

"In the castle? Absurd! Just how would they get in the castle?"

"Well, we got a door..."

"Yes, a door that is heavily fortified with a drawbridge that raises up to seal the door!"

"That reminds me," said Fiddius, who had been pondering a question for some time now, but had never quite remembered to ask it. "What's the point of that drawbridge, anyway? We ain't even got a moat."

A moat! Sir Bimmiden slapped his hand to his forehead in anguish. Of course! His castle needed a moat! A great, wide moat full of crocodiles and man-eating fish and any number of deadly waterfowl! That was what would make the castle *really* safe! He made a mental note to have Fiddius begin digging in the morning. "Yes, we shall have a moat. But now, back to my original point," he said, trying to get back to his original point. "Why haven't we been attacked?" Fiddius began intensely studying something on his left shoe and shrugged his great, broad shoulders. "I don't know either," murmured Bimmiden, almost to himself. He returned to the window and resumed his forlorn position. "All right," he said, careful not to let his chin rest too long on the cold stone for any solid length of time, "why do castles fall under attack?"

Fiddius shifted his weight uneasily in his small wooden chair. He was not used to having to answer so many questions in one day. "Siege on the kingdom?" he asked.

"Yes! Siege on the kingdom. That's one. Now technically, we belong to the kingdom of Camelot, do we not?" An exaggerated nod from Fiddius. "And Camelot is the greatest and most glorious kingdom in the world, is it not?" And another. "Then it would be reasonable to suppose that Arthur has probably managed to collect quite a few adversaries out of jealousy, would it not?" Fiddius' head was now in a constant bob. "Then it would be logical that someone might try to take over this kingdom, despite its obvious strength, because, as we all know, jealousy is a rather blinding motive. And if someone were to lay siege on the kingdom, it would also be logical to start with our castle, right?" Fiddius' head stopped bouncing.

"Would it?"

"Of course it would! We're the farthest out from Camelot and by far the smallest. Right? So we'd be the easiest to conquer. Or," he added with a knowing little chuckle, "so said opponent would *think*. Little would he know that he would be facing two of Arthur's most decorated Knights of the Round Table. Ha *ha*!"

"Actually," Fiddius pointed out, rather unhelpfully, "we're not really part of the Round Table, are we?"

"Well… no, not as such." Bimmiden deflated slightly. "But! If the Table suffered a handful of losses in battle, say six or seven men, I'm sure we'd be considered to fill their spots. So… we're more like the most decorated Knights of the Small Parlor Table in the Anteroom Adjacent to the Room Which Holds the Round Table."

"We're not decorated, either."

"Not *yet*, you mean. We're not decorated *yet*. Once we defend this castle from vicious onslaught, there will be no end to our commendations!"

"But this castle ain't bein' onslaughted."

"Yes, of course, that's my point, you bumbling fool!" Bimmiden exploded. "How are we to become the most decorated Knights of the Small Parlor Anteroom Table if no one lays siege to our castle?!" He resumed his pacing. He was feeling very high-strung this morning. "If they were to lay siege to Arthur's kingdom, as already discussed, they would undoubtedly start with our castle. Right?"

"Right," agreed Fiddius, quickly becoming lost in Bimmiden's pea soup of logic.

"Right. Then we can assume that the kingdom of Camelot is not under siege, because we are not under attack. We may strike that from the list. Why else might a castle fall under attack?"

Fiddius was well over his head at this point and silently wished to return to his chessboard, but there was no stopping Bimmiden when he got his dander up like this. He resumed thinking. "Maybe… maybe… revenge?" he asked, hitting upon a rare gem of an idea.

"Yes, of course, revenge! We might be attacked in order to have vengeance wrought upon us by an opposing faction! Yes. That's good. Maybe we can work with that. How many enemies do you have?"

Fiddius looked up in surprise. "Who, me?"

"Yes, of course you! Who else?!"

"I ain't got no enemies, Sir Bimmiden."

"Hmm. No, I don't suppose you do."

"I don't like to interfere with other people's business."

"No, nor I," mused Bimmiden. "There was that one fellow I

bumped into at the market two weeks ago. Remember? I stepped on his foot by accident?"

"Oh, yes, I remember that," said Fiddius cheerfully. Rare moments of distinct memory were always a cause for joy.

"He might come looking for vengeance, I suppose."

"I thought that's what he did when he socked you in the nose, right there and then."

"Yes. I suppose you're right." Bimmiden tenderly touched his nose in memory of the encounter. It still throbbed every now and again. "All right, so we can rule out vengeance. Why else might someone try to take our castle?"

"Maybe... maybe for fun?" suggested Fiddius, who was obviously out of ideas.

Bimmiden had not considered this as an option and found himself weighing this possibility in his mind. "Why, yes, Sir Fiddius, perhaps... perhaps we might be attacked some day for the sheer fun of it! Why, I've heard tell of such rascally rogues that might just try such a trick! Like... like the Red Knight of Capperdom! He's known for his cruel, mistempered onslaughts, isn't he? He might be just the type to attack a small castle simply for the fun of it! Perhaps we should send word to him, taunt him a little, see if he bites. Where do you suppose he lives?"

"I don't know," replied Fiddius, who really did not know. "Capperdom?"

"Hmm. Yes, he just might. That's it! We'll write to the Red Knight and provoke his anger. Ha *ha*! Sir Fiddius, fetch hither the parchment and quill!"

"Fetch it wither?"

"Hither!"

"Thither?"

"Yes, yes, hither!"

Fiddius trotted toward the stairwell, which led to the chamber where the paper was generally kept, but stopped himself before leaving the common room. "Oh. Ah... we ain't got no more parchment."

"What do you mean we ain't got no more parchment? We had a full stock last week!"

"Yes, well, I've been making these little parchment boats that we could float around in a moat if we ever got one," he said, producing a small, hastily folded piece of parchment that looked very much like it would never float. "And now, we're getting one!" he added happily.

Bimmiden found himself turning a rather deep shade of crimson. "Then find me something else to write on!"

"Okay. Oh, ah… but we ain't got no more quills, neither."

"You can't be serious! We had at least three good quills as of yesterday. I checked! What have you done with them?"

"*What I do with quills in my own time is my own business!*" Fiddius exploded in an unprecedented fit of rage. Bimmiden, literally taken aback by this show of emotion, stumbled backward into the wall. Another piece of stone crumbled to the floor. "All right then," he assented rather shakily. "We'll forget the Red Knight."

Fiddius, who was breathing abnormally from the strain of his outburst, sat down to steady himself. When he spoke again, it was in his normal, sweet, slightly oafish voice. "Do you think…" he began with what was apparently an original thought, which obviously lent itself to a long pause and some careful mulling. "Do you think… maybe… we're here, at this castle, the farthest castle from Camelot and the smallest of all castles… maybe… to keep us out of the way?"

"Preposterous! What an insult that you would even think such a thing! For shame! Why would you possibly think that?"

"Well, because I don't think Arthur was very happy with the whole dragon situation—"

"I've told you time and time again, we shan't discuss the dragon situation!" cried Bimmiden. He flung himself into the chair opposite Fiddius, crossed his arms on the table, and buried his face in them. The pain of his shame was far too great to bear.

"It's just that Arthur was really quite upset over the whole thing."

"I said we shan't talk about it!" came the muffled cry.

"Yes, but what I'm saying is, when you're fighting a dragon, you're supposed to *save* the damsel in distress, not throw her to the dragon as a diversion."

"It was either her or me!" yelled Bimmiden, jumping up from his chair and once again resuming his pacing. "That thing had massive teeth, I mean—" He made an exaggeratedly large gesture with his hands. "And how am I supposed to serve Arthur on the Round Table if I'm eaten by a bloody dragon? Tell me that!"

"I don't think that's the point," said Fiddius, not entirely sure what the point really was.

"It is *precisely* the point!" insisted Bimmiden. "Furthermore, I am thoroughly convinced that the world is a happier place without that screeching wench! Damsel, indeed! If her father hadn't been the king of some French province or other, there's no way she'd have been—" Here, he was interrupted with a pounding from below. His heart leapt into his throat. "Sir Fiddius! Did you hear that?"

"I did. I think someone's at the door."

"Perhaps we are under attack! Ha *ha*!" He yanked his sword from its hilt and whirled it about his head. This caused him to falter and crash against the stone wall. It, of course, let loose some chalky fragments. The weight of the sword always took him by surprise, but he rebounded easily. "Grab your longsword, Sir Fiddius! Ready the cooking staff! Our triumph is at hand!" And with that, he dashed down the stairs to tangle with fate.

Sir Fiddius sat in his chair, scratching his head. It was almost lunchtime, and interrupting the cooking staff now would mean a delay in his early afternoon meal. Defending the castle was certainly important, but he had missed breakfast that morning, as he had opted instead to ready his fleet of parchment boats in case the castle somehow sprang a leak – a preparation he did not regret making, especially now that a moat had been promised. It had, however, left him quite hungry, and he didn't think he could survive until lunch if it were to be delayed. He therefore decided not to ready the cooking staff for battle and instead descended the steps alone in the wake of his fellow knight.

Bimmiden raced to the drawbridge, sword in hand, knocking it about on walls and doorways as he went. When he finally reached the heavy wooden door, he was out of breath and had to take a few moments to compose himself. The pounding from the other side of the bridge continued impatiently. "Hello in there!" called a forceful voice. "Open this door! I demand that you open this door!"

"Come to face your death, have you?!" cried Bimmiden. "Come to take this castle, eh? Well, give it your all, you sodden-faced kneebenders! Send your army crashing to its death against these fortified stone walls of steel!"

"I don't have an army, you silly twit, and I'm not here to take your castle. I come in the name of King Arthur. Now let me in."

Bimmiden puzzled at this. "You're not here to lay siege on the kingdom?"

"Of course not," called the voice from without. "Who in his right mind would try to take this silly castle? This entire area is wholly inconsequential! Now, are you going to let me in, or must I enter by force?"

By this time, Fiddius had heaved his way to the drawbridge, and he stood behind Bimmiden, panting mightily. "Who is it?" he gasped.

"I don't know," replied Bimmiden. He pressed closer to the door. "Who are you?"

"I am Lancelot du Lake, highest Knight of King Arthur's Round Table, and I demand that you let me in!"

Bimmiden started with surprise. He turned to Fiddius. "It's Lancelot!"

"Lancelot? You mean, *the* Lancelot?"

"Yes, you idiot, *the* Lancelot!"

"What do you think he's doing here?"

"How do I know? Come… come to take us back to Camelot, I suppose!"

"Gor!" breathed Fiddius in awe. "Do you think so?"

"I don't know, I don't know, just… make a good impression, all right?"

"Right."

"Have you bathed today?"

"I ain't bathed in months," answered Fiddius truthfully.

"Bloody hell!"

"Look!" came the now terribly impatient cry from the other side of the drawbridge. "If you do not open this door immediately, I shall gain entry by force, and probably severely wound several of you in the process, and that shall make me very put out!"

"Well, what are you waiting for?" snapped Bimmiden. "Open the door!" Fiddius jogged over to the hand crank and began lowering the drawbridge. Before it was halfway down, Lancelot leapt impatiently through the widening crack between wood and wall and came to a sliding halt in the castle's main hall. Bimmiden noticed, to his embarrassment, that the contrast between the most famous of knights and himself couldn't be more obvious. Whereas Lancelot was clean and wearing a spotless purple cloak, Bimmiden was streaked with grime and mold from head to foot. While Lancelot smelled like almonds and cloves, Bimmiden smelled like something else entirely. And Lancelot's hair – his brilliant, flaxen, blond hair – seemed to shine and glitter, despite the severe lack of light present inside the castle. Bimmiden's hair was so caked with dirt the original color could hardly be determined.

Needless to say, he was greatly humbled.

"Lancelot!" he yelped in a voice much higher than normal, trying to remain cool under the circumstances. "What brings you to humble Castle Dim?" Fiddius, on signal from Bimmiden, began to backtrack his cranking, bringing the drawbridge back to a close.

"No, no, that won't be necessary," said Lancelot, stopping Fiddius mid-crank. "I won't be staying long. I'm here by order of King Arthur."

"I knew it! You're here to bring us back to Camelot!" exclaimed Bimmiden. He flushed with memories of the gleaming white castle, its unfurled crimson banners, its lavish parties, its wide, decadent moat…

"What? Oh, no, no, no!" said Lancelot, laughing heartily. "Lord, no. Ha ha! No. Nothing like that, of course. No, you see, the king's cooking staff had an unfortunate row with a kitchen fire, and they perished all in the flames, and so, you see, we need a *new* cooking staff, and the king figured, why waste a good three-person staff on a two-knight castle? So it's actually your cooking staff I'll be taking back to Camelot. You two are to remain here and… keep up the good fight." He pumped a hearty fist into the air in a well-practiced show of honor and solidarity. Then he went up to the kitchen, gathered the cooking staff – who were, it is fair to say, more than slightly cheered by this unexpected visit – and ushered the entire beaming crew out of the miserable castle. Then the golden-haired knight turned back to the castle's tenants and, deciding not to shake hands, saluted them sharply. "Well, gents," he said. "Back to work." And he was gone.

Bimmiden and Fiddius stood in the half-open doorway, stupefied. They had just simultaneously lost both their kitchen staff and more than half of their army. Just how the devil were they to become decorated Knights of the Anteroom now? Bimmiden had a sneaking suspicion that perhaps some greater plan was at work here, and that maybe it did have something to do with the dragon incident after all. The pieces of some sort of puzzle were pinging around in his mind, but he couldn't quite manage to fit them together. Fiddius, meanwhile, had a far greater concern on his mind.

"Does this mean that lunch will be delayed?"

"Oh, shut up, you stupid sod," said Bimmiden, giving Fiddius a hefty smack across the arm with the blade of his sword. "Go dig your stupid moat." This cheered Fiddius somewhat, because the thought of his parchment boats being permanently landlocked in his chamber above was quite disheartening. And so he spent the next several months digging a healthy-sized moat while Bimmiden trained himself in the fine art of reducing full meals to cinders. Thus they lived in their small castle on the edge of Arthur's kingdom, surrounded by a moat, which, they quickly realized, was not to be properly utilized, as they had no means to fill it with water, much less with crocodiles or man-eating fish or any number of deadly water fowl. But it was a mighty ditch and certainly would have caused any number of attackers to stumble slightly upon advancement, and that was something. And eventually, the inhabitants of Castle Dim *did* prove their worth in battle, to a certain extent. But that, dear reader, is another story for perhaps another day.

The Saloon at the Edge of Gehenna
(A Story in Three Parts)

Part I: The Cowboy and the Spaceman

"Save yer spit for the desert 'tween Mad Margie's legs, Simpson. I'll shine my own glass," the old cowboy muttered, stubbing his gnarled finger against the top of the bar like a spent cigar. The bartender checked the glob of mucus clinging to the top of his throat and swallowed it with a grimace. He slammed the dirty glass down in front of the cowboy, which nearly broke the old man's finger. "I'll shine my own glass," the cowboy repeated, his bushy mustache covering a sly grin. "There's bits in yer spit're like to do more harm than a glass full of this rat-shit dust clot. Consumption 'n' fever 'n' God knows what itching, scabbed up split ye've been divin' intuh." He huffed at the glass, his breath raspy and wet. He gave a guttural choke, and up came his own thick, pale glob of spit. He coughed it into the glass and wiped it around the sides with the hem of his dusty shirt. When he was finished, the glass was smeared, filthier than it had been before. "There!" he cried happily, pushing his floppy old hat back higher on his head. "Now she's ready!"

Simpson shook his head and pulled the cork from the unmarked bottle on the shelf. "You bring money today?" he asked, his voice tired.

"I bring money every day," the old man said defensively.

"You haven't brought money in three years."

"I bring joy to yer god-ridden puss. What better payment could a child of the Earth ask for?" He grabbed the glass with a shaky hand, spilling brown drops over his knuckles, and slammed it against his open mouth. The whiskey went down his throat without his even having to swallow. "'Nother."

Just as Simpson went to refill the glass, the saloon's batwing doors squeaked open, and a man walked into the bar. Well, perhaps it was a man, and perhaps it wasn't.

"Jerkin' Jesus," the old cowboy exclaimed. "What in desperation's cove is this, now?"

The being that might have been a man looked around the room. Nearly every table in the place was empty, but he settled his sights on a barstool, despite the obvious awkwardness of his sitting on one. He tottered over to the bar, dragged back a stool, and hoisted himself up onto it with surprising grace. His white suit crinkled like newspaper against the wood as he situated himself. Then he just sat, arms crossed on the bar, and stared at the bottles on the shelf.

Simpson eyed him nervously. He waited for an order. But the being that might have been a man just sat, staring quietly. Or maybe he wasn't staring. Maybe he didn't have anything to stare with. It was impossible to tell.

The old cowboy looked down the bar with rare surprise. The being that might have been a man sat still as stone. The cowboy slapped his withered palms against the edge of the bar. "I give up!" he cried, flinging his head back for effect. Little drips of whiskey flew off his mangy mustache and flecked Simpson's clean-shaven chin. "What are ya?"

The being that might have been a man turned his whole body very slowly around to face the cowboy. This was a fairly impressive feat, given the white suit's constricting nature. But spin it did, all the way around until it sat facing the cowboy's stool dead on, and the cowboy got a good look at the creature's get-up. The suit was a full body, crinkly white thing with arms and legs like a flattened out accordion. It was bulky, or maybe the thing wearing it was bulky, in all the wrong places. It bore a series of red and blue squares on the chest that served no utility as far as the cowboy could tell. And there was a flag stitched on the sleeve, a flag with the same colors of America's flag, but with a different design. It had stripes. No, the being that might have been a man sure wasn't from around here.

He wore boots on his feet, but not any kind of boot the cowboy had ever seen. Not pointed and heeled, but round and flat from end to end, like short, sandpapered fence posts. He wore gloves – big gloves, white and crinkly like his suit – fixed to his sleeves with some sort of metal band. Each of his fingers was the size of a donkey's prick in heat. He wore a giant white box on his back with tubes and wires poking out of it every which way, most of them leading up to the great globe of a helmet that sat on the creature's head. The helmet was the real kicker: It was perfectly spherical and bigger than a fishbowl. And shiny! Lord, the damned thing was more reflective than any mirror. The cowboy could see his own wizened face in its surface from halfway across the bar. It practically radiated with love of reflecting things.

The being that might have been a man put his finger to one of the red squares on his chest. Something inside the suit coughed to life and emitted a buzz like a hive of angry bees trapped in burlap. Then a voice emerged from the same, hidden place. It was as crackly and electric as lightning.

I am a spaceman.

"So y'are a man," the cowboy said, satisfied.

"A human man?" Simpson asked, chewing his lip nervously. And of course this was a logical question, perhaps *the* logical question, despite how ridiculous it may have sounded. The last time he had demurred from asking someone whether or not he was a human man, the saloon had ended up half blown to hell, one-quarter burned, and all the way covered in three inches of purple goo that smelled like a dead and rotting possum. Now, any time there was doubt, he just asked if the person was human.

The man who might have been a human pressed the red square on his chest again. Again, the static and the crackling voice: *Of course.*

"Why you wearin' that looking glass on yer head? Whyn't you take it off, if yer a human man?"

The spaceman shook with laughter. At least, they assumed it was laughter. He was either laughing or having a seizure. Without the red square depressed, they couldn't tell for sure.

Because this 'looking glass' on my head is the only thing keeping me alive, he said when he finally did press the square.

"You got a condition?" Simpson asked, trying to look nonchalant. But of course, he wasn't nonchalant. The last time someone had walked into his bar with "a condition," the whole place had to go into quarantine for 6 weeks, and Simpson himself got treated to a humiliating public delousing in Gus Cormer's horse troughs. Now, any time there was doubt, he just asked if the person had a condition.

I have no condition, the voice crackled. He sat quiet for a moment. *Well. I might be coming down with a cold. A great nuisance. But no, I do not have a 'condition.'* Simpson exhaled in relief, then wandered off to spit in some more glasses. The evening rush would be starting soon.

"If ya ain't got a condition, whyn't you take off yer shiny hat? What's the matter with ya?" the cowboy demanded.

It is not what is the matter with me. It is what is the matter with you.

"What is what's the matter with me?"

The spaceman paused. His bulbous helmet tilted down at the floor, and his finger touched the gleaming surface lightly. Finally, he said, *I do not know how to answer that question.*

"Why not?"

Its syntax is… confusing.

"Simpson! Leave a bottle." Extensive vocabularies in others

caused a strong want of drink in the cowboy. The bartender reappeared with a murky bottle of whiskey in hand and set it in front of the cowboy. Then he rushed back to his row of glasses at the other end of the bar. He had a very good clod of mucus worked up in his throat, and he didn't want to waste it.

To answer your original question, the spaceman continued, *I cannot remove my helmet because I would instantly suffocate in your atmosphere.*

"That don't make sense."

It makes perfect sense.

"I breathe the air ever' day. I ain't died yet."

Yes. That is curious, the spaceman mused. *Clearly a genetic defect native to this dust bowl. Or perhaps an ingested anomaly. Some sort of organic, fibrous resin in the water supply. Saves you from the toxins in the atmosphere, but slowly coats your lungs over time. I'd wager you lose thousands per year to suffocation.* The cowboy shook his head irritably. He grew tired of this talk. *You'll suffocate any minute now, I suppose,* the spaceman continued, heedless. *What a privilege and a horror, to witness such an act of an abhorrent Nature.*

"What's yer drink?" the cowboy muttered, a desperate plea to find other ways for the man to occupy his mouth.

Ah. Yes. What do you have that's light and crisp, bartender?

"I got whiskey," Simpson said. His voice was now choked and dry and absent of mucus. But the glasses were especially clean.

Yes, I'm sure. But something else, I think. Pomberry spirits? An Elysian brand, perhaps? Simpson raised an eyebrow uncertainly. He looked at the cowboy, who could only shrug and take a long pull straight from his bottle. Simpson frowned at the newcomer. "No pombrey spirits, friend. No Elees—Ellie—none of that other, neither." The spaceman considered this. He tapped a heavily gloved finger thoughtfully against his glass helmet. Then he touched the red square again. *A jewel flower liqueur, perhaps?* Simpson shook his head. *Turnabout blossom wine?* No. *Tonic of Etheria?* No. *Evergreen mash?* No. *Then how about caper ale? Surely you must have caper ale.*

"I got whiskey," the bartender repeated with the practiced patience of a master of his profession. "I got it strong, and I got it blind-eye, and I got it stronger. I got a couple bottles of Mitch Dawson's homebrew. No idea what to call it, but it ain't jewel flower, it ain't evergreen, and it ain't no wine. It's rotgut. Rotgut or whiskey: Which'll ya have?"

The spaceman sat straight and still and considered. Finally, he touched his voice square and said, *I bet you have corporal nectar, though. Yes?*

The cowboy lolled his head back, then slammed it against the bar. He just didn't know what else to do. Simpson was going to kill this foreigner. His head planted firmly on the rough wood of the bar, he slid his six-shooter out of the holster at his right hip and held it up toward the bartender, grip first.

But Simpson was a professional. Appease the customer, contain the situation. That was his motto. Or it would have been, were he given to a slightly higher vocabulary. Keep the crazy bastard calm, he thought in the parlance of his own mind. He nodded amiably and said, "Sure, we got that corkel nectar. Sure we do. Damn, slipped my mind." The spaceman raised his hands in a silent cheer, and Simpson made a big show of digging around behind the bar and plucking out an especially dusty, especially labelless bottle from the very back of the stock. He slammed the bottle down on the bar. A thick coating of pale brown dirt puffed out and sifted onto the bar, the floor, and the spaceman's gloves. Simpson grabbed a recently shined shot glass, pulled out the cork (with no small amount of effort), and sloshed the glass full to the brim. He slid it across the bar to the spaceman. "The best corkel nectar we got. Won't find its like nowhere else, guaranteed."

The spaceman stared at the glass. The mirrored globe on his head tilted to one side, then to the other. He pressed his red square. *The color looks about right.* Even through the crackling, his voice was heavy with doubt. "Course it looks 'bout right," Simpson said indignantly, shocked beyond belief that the color looked anything even approaching "right." "Two bits."

The spaceman fumbled at a zipper on his right sleeve. His padded sausage fingers made it impossible to grip the little metal pull. *Excuse me*, he said, leaning toward the cowboy. *Could you help me with this?* The cowboy grumbled something under his breath and leaned over to inspect the zipper. It seemed safe enough. But in this town, in this world, with strangers like this, well, hell, you just never knew. He grabbed for his hat and held it out next to the spaceman's arm, the crown of the hat pointing back at the cowboy, as if the leather cup could shield him from whatever nuclear explosive he might trip in the spaceman's suit. Then, with the other hand, he grasped the zipper and gave it a hard yank.

Thank you, strange man, the spaceman said. "Yer welcome, stranger. Thankee fer not blowin' me to bits." The spaceman tipped his head graciously. Then he reached into the sleeve pocket and retrieved a small fold of faded green paper. *Do you have change for twenty, bartender?*

"Twenty what?" Simpson asked, frowning at the bill held forth by the astronaut. He plucked it from the outstretched glove and examined it closely. It was no money he'd ever seen before – it had a Zyrgian pyramid printed on one side and the portrait of some bearded man named Reynolds on the other – but it was by no means the most outlandish currency he'd ever accepted. Strange it may be, but at least it wasn't glowing with radiation or, as far as he could tell, printed with blood. And it was far lighter than Gehenna's own lead coins and would be easier to conceal when he walked, so what the hell. He shrugged and dropped the bill into the cardboard cash box by the seltzer bottle. He fished around and retrieved a small, hard-plastic cube with the figure "$50" stamped on all six sides and slid it to the spaceman.

What's this?

"Yer change. Fifty."

The spaceman examined it through his mirrored helmet. *Fifty what?*

"Lemme ask you somethin'," piped up the cowboy, who had begun feeling ignored. "You gon' take off yer helmet?" The spaceman shook his head. "Then how you plan on enjoyin' that liver-eater?" he asked, pointing to the shot glass. The spaceman raised one finger, as if he'd just been stricken by a wonderful idea. He pressed a small blue square on the chest of his suit. A little hatch flipped open on his left arm near the wrist. He leaned over to give the cowboy a good look at the inner workings of the sleeve. The cowboy peered down and saw a series of tiny straw-like tubes running along beneath the outer layer. One tube, bent up at a right angle, was topped with a miniature funnel. The spaceman pointed at the funnel, then traced his finger up his arm, all the way to the spot on his helmet that was probably covering his mouth. Then he tapped this spot a few times as if to say, *It goes in my mouth.* The cowboy shook his head. "Hell. I prefer the ol' fashion way." He proved it with another slug from his bottle.

The spaceman picked up his glass and held it aloft. He spun around (inasmuch as the suit would allow it) and saluted everyone in the bar. Then he dumped the entire contents into the funnel and shut the hatch.

The cowboy acknowledged the salute and went back about his business of obliterating his senses. The bar was still for a moment; the cowboy sipped, the bartender wiped, the patrons drank, and the spaceman sat. But only for a moment. For as soon as that one moment passed, the spaceman jerked his limbs like a cat on a slack line. He stumbled back, knocking his stool to the floor, and stutter-shuffled to the middle of the room. He waved his arms wildly and jumped up and down. He jerked around the room like a man on fire, but because of the helmet, all of this was done in complete silence. The cowboy screwed up his face in confusion. "What the hell's he doin'?"

"I think he just found out we don't serve corkel nectar."

The spaceman's finger found the little red square. *Water! Wa-*

ter! He crackled. He threw his arms out and made a mad dash for the bar. Simpson, alarmed, grabbed for a pitcher and dipped it full from the wash sink. He set it on the bar just as the spaceman collided into the rail. He yanked the pitcher up and poured it over the hatch in his arm, but the hatch was still closed. He fumbled with the squares on his chest until he found the right one. The hatch popped, but he still couldn't pour the water in fast enough. In a burst of desperation, his chest heaved hugely, then, with both hands, he unlocked his helmet and popped it from his head. It clattered to the floor, revealing a clean-shaven, red-faced (and human-looking) man with closely cropped black hair. His cheeks were puffed, swollen with held air. He opened his mouth and poured the water from the pitcher straight down his gullet. It splashed over his face, drenching his nose and chin in thick, brown rivulets. He squeezed his eyes shut and shook his head violently, then spat the dirty water back out onto the bar. He exhaled in a long explosion, scrambled on the floor for his helmet, and made a series of desperate whimpers as he secured it back on his head. It locked into place, and the spaceman slumped against his overturned stool, his chest rising and falling faster than a quarter horse's after the Ploughman Race.

The cowboy snorted. "That's why I do it the ol' fashion way."

The spaceman slowly collected himself. He stood up, a little shaky, and pulled his stool back to an upright position. He mounted it, shook his head a few times, and took a deep breath. Then he tapped a finger down on the bar next to his glass. *I'll have another,* he crackled.

The cowboy grinned. "Partner, this one's on me."

Part II: Them Snot-Nosed, Slick-Shit Poofs

"Ahls tell you one thing," the cowboy slurred, clutching blindly at his third bottle. "No man'll ever go to the stars."

I'm telling you, crackled the spaceman, who was still struggling happily with his first bottle of whatever it was that wasn't corporal nectar. *I've been to the stars. I've set foot on 18—no, wait!—21 stars. Let's see. Betelgeuse, Polaris, Detrius-12, Sadalbari, Beta Core D, Sugarsprive, Deneb... well, Deneb twice. Alsafi, Pollux, Wasat, Cursa-4, Grey Nookie, Blue Nookie, Ash Nookie, Nookie Red, Zaurak, Zautak, Tarzak, Zartauk, Karzaut, and Cor Caroli. 21 stars.* His voice crackled with pride.

The cowboy looked at him over his drooping mustache. "What were that 17th one again?"

The spaceman threw up his hands and held them there like two surprised prairie dogs. Then he began to count inside his helmet, ticking them off on his fingers as he went. His head bobbed side to side with each tick, and four times he got stuck and had to start up again. The cowboy gleefully reached over and pushed the spaceman's red talking square. The astronaut was in such a concentrated flurry, he didn't even notice. *Betelgeuse, Polaris, Detrius-12, Deneb—no, Alsafi—wait. Betelgeuse, Polaris, Beta Core D—wait. BetelgeusePolarisDetrius-12BetaCoreD...* he rattled off in a crackling whisper. The cowboy laughed a laugh that was rough as gravel and twice as dry. "I'm jus' spinnin' yer lasso, pardner. I do believe you did set foot on 21 o' them stars. What're they like?"

Surprisingly brisk, for giant balls of burning gas. We lost a lot of men to hypothermia on the stars.

"Well, here's to 'em," the cowboy said, raising his bottle. The spaceman raised his in turn, they clacked them together, and then they each tipped back: the cowboy to his lips, the spaceman to his funnel.

"Say, how ya piss in that thing?" the cowboy asked, nodding at the suit.

The spaceman stopped pouring and straightened the bottle. He took a second to think, then said simply, *That's a different funnel.*

"Eyes up," Simpson whispered from across the bar. He nodded toward the front of the bar. A man pushed through the batwings, talking excitedly and laughing to another man and a woman who followed close behind. The spaceman couldn't quite place it, but there was something strange about the crew. Their clothes were a little out of place, but that wasn't it. Blazes, as if he were one to talk! His government-issued extravehicular mobility unit with its Primary Life-Support System and airtight helmet, completely electroplated with 24-karat gold, didn't exactly blend in among the denim and chaps. No, the newcomers looked more at home here than he did, that's for sure. But, something...

"Heyo, barkeep!" one of the men chirped. He was tall and muscular, and his arms were lean, but not ropy like those of the cattle herders staring at them squint-eyed from around the room. His blond hair was messy but oiled; he must have spent twenty minutes wrestling each lock into perfectly catastrophic asymmetry. He wore blue jeans, like most of the bar's patrons, though his weren't caked with dirt and grease. In fact, they looked freshly cleaned, crisply pressed. He wore a white linen shirt with the sleeves rolled up and with just enough buttons undone to give a glimpse of a strong, tanned, hairless chest pumping beneath the thin material. He had a jawline like a chrome bumper, and the only blemish on his otherwise angelic face was one long scar, faded by the years but kept pink by the sun, that ran down his left cheek just under his eye. He had a leather satchel slung over his shoulder so that the strap crossed his torso from shoulder to hip. The leather was cracked and weathered, but well-oiled for its age. "What do you have that's adventurous?" he asked with a grin.

"If it's from this bar and yer drinkin' it, it's adventurous," said Simpson stiffly. "How many?"

"One for each, I think," the blond man said, still smiling his smooth smile. "Unless anyone objects." He turned to his band of merry wanderers for their approval.

The second man was clad in navy blue dress pants and a white, short-sleeved, button-down shirt with a blue epaulette on each shoulder and a golden pin fashioned to look like wings fixed just above his breast pocket. He carried a stiff blue cap under one arm and wore ridiculously oversized darkened lenses over his eyes, despite the sparse candlelight of the saloon. "Fine by me," he said, chomping on something squishy between his molars. Gum, the spaceman thought. Cud, figured the cowboy.

The two men were undoubtedly dapper, and certainly not displeasing to the eye, but it was the woman who drew the attention (and the collective breath) of the room. She was olive-skinned and tall and possessed a reedy slenderness that didn't emphasize her flat stomach quite as much as it did her well-placed and expansive curves. She had slipped her way into a shimmering blue dress that molded perfectly to her exquisite form. It was floor-length, with a long slit in the left side that traipsed up her thigh and tapered to a seam high on her hip. It was the sort of slit a man might give himself over to boiling for, if he weren't careful.

The hem of the dress splayed delicately across the floorboards around her feet, which she had slipped gracefully into a pair of diamond-studded silver heels. She wore deep-green jewels at her wrist and on a long necklace that settled in the downy softness where her chest began its declarative ascent. On her head she had placed a delicate tiara, silver with white diamonds bordering the same emeralds as those at her wrist and bosom. Her jewels drank in the flickering light and reflected it tenfold through the shadowy saloon. Her eyes, green jewels themselves, flashed with the same dazzling brightness.

"Oooo, a saloon adventure in the lonesome West! How delightful!" she cried, clapping her gloved hands together cheerfully.

"Three," counted Simpson, the consummate professional. "Comin' right up."

"Bring them over when they're ready, will ya, pal?" the blond one asked. "And heck, bring the whole bottle." The woman cried out as if this were the most tremendously wonderful idea she'd heard all day. The trio waltzed over to an empty table between two sets of blackened miners and sat down, looking perfectly at ease with their current stations.

"IFs," the cowboy grumbled. "Bet yer too-chapped ass."

The spaceman leaned forward on his stool. *I'm sorry, IFs?*

"You got ears on that helmet? IFs, IFs!"

The spaceman searched his memory for a correlating definition of the word "if" used as a noun and came up blank. He keyed a neat little pattern into the buttons on his chest, and the mini hard drive stored somewhere in the giant PLSS pack on his back whirred to life and whispered into the microphone in his ear: *Command.* "Return all definitions for the word 'if,'" the spaceman said into the small microphone in his helmet. Without pressing the speaker button, of course, the cowboy couldn't hear the conversation between man and machine that was going on inside the suit, and he stared blankly at his new friend, wondering if he'd perhaps suffered a sudden stroke.

The computer whirred some more, and then it clicked. *If. Conjunction. Definition alpha: In the event that, allowing that, on the assumption that, or on condition that. Definition beta: Whether. Definition gamma: even though, although perhaps. Definition delta: And perhaps not even, on the contrary even, perhaps even. End of entry. Command.* The spaceman shook his head and pressed his voice-box button. *I don't know a single correlating definition for the use of the word 'if' as a noun.* The cowboy blinked. A sea of bewilderment crashed down upon him. The spaceman saw him drowning and threw out a lifeline: *What the hell is an IF?*

"What're you, a scrat?" the cowboy laughed, throwing his head back and slapping the bar. His mustache came to life and danced a jig on his upper lip. "We ain't had a scrat in these parts fer at least twenty turns!"

What is a scrat? the spaceman asked, suddenly feeling very self-conscious. He possessed a Bachelor of Science degree, a Bachelor of Mathematical Logic degree, a Master of Rocket Theory degree, two Master of Outer-Limit Space degrees (one emphasizing Intergalactic Mineral Compositions, the other focusing on Deep

Vacuum Physics), a Doctorate in Advanced Thermalgenesis, and a Doctorate in Tenth-Quadrant String Theory Acceleration, but he had never, ever heard the word "scrat," and he had been almost positive the word "if" had no noun form. Perhaps, he thought, I should have taken an English Lit course somewhere in there.

"A fish outta water, ya might say," the cowboy grinned. "Hey, ever'body!" he cried, lifting his glass to the entire room. "The spaceman here is a bona fide scrat!"

"MAZEL TOV!" the room exclaimed in unison. Each man, woman, and child (yes, the spaceman now saw, there were three children sipping on beer bottles in the corner) raised a glass high in the air, clinked it against its neighbors, slammed it thrice on the table, and threw back a mighty swig.

The spaceman was glad to be wearing the helmet. Not only was it protecting him from the poisonous local atmosphere, but more importantly, it was hiding the red flares of embarrassment that now flushed his cheeks. The cowboy leaned in conspiratorially. "Lemme ask ya, scrat. How long've you known whatcha are?"

In terms of what? the spaceman asked indignantly.

The cowboy grinned, and the spaceman caught sight of a solid-gold molar pushing up from the man's chaw-stained gums. "Ya know what I mean."

The spaceman sighed. He supposed he did know. In fact, he could recall perfectly the moment he realized the truth about himself and yet could not accurately measure the time that had passed since that moment. *I'm not sure. Time... works differently now.*

"Time always worked differ'ntly. Ya jus' didn't notice it."

But before, days were... days. One day lasted 27 hours, and that was that. Here, each day is a month.

"10 hours, on a long one," the cowboy corrected. "Come Ragmuss Day, they kin settle down to 30 minutes all told."

It's enough to drive a person to drink. The spaceman punctuated this sentiment by tipping the last of his whiskey into his wrist funnel. He signaled Simpson for another bottle; the bartender already had it waiting.

"Don' let that old fucker step-dance 'round your brain too hard, son," the bartender said, pulling the cork and setting the bottle in front of the astronaut. "He's jus' old, tiresome, and cranky to boot. An IF is an Imaginary Friend."

"It's an acrimony," the cowboy agreed.

An acronym, you mean. The spaceman sat and twiddled with the new bottle, spinning it carefully, watching the rotgut inside wash up the curved glass neck. *Technically speaking, aren't we all imaginary friends?*

The cowboy guffawed. "Son, you got a lot to learn," he drawled. "We may be imaginary, sure as shit, but we wasn't dreamed up to be nobody's friend. Take Simpson 'n' me, here. We wasn't made fer friends. I ain't never met a real-life Anchor. Neither's Simpson."

"You don't know what I've done with my life, y'old sot," Simpson said. "What do you think I do when you lot leave? Stand here and wait fer mornin' so's I kin open back up and pour whiskey down yer sorry throats?"

"Well, have ya?"

"Have I what?"

"Ever met a real-life Anchor?"

"It just so happens I have not."

"Then stop jawin' and lemme finish."

What's an Anchor? the spaceman interrupted.

"Christ, a real scrat," the cowboy sneered, finishing off his second bottle.

"An Anchor is a person, an honest-to-goodness, real-life, real-world person who dreams up imaginaries like us," Simpson explained, grabbing a new bottle for the cowboy. He held it up against the gas-jet flames in the chandelier and inspected the murky brown liquid. "Got some tobacco wrappers floatin' in this one, G.W. Charge ya half for it."

"Charge me nothin' fer it, ya crook," the cowboy said, snatching the bottle from the bartender's hands. "Whose tobacco?"

"That bottle came from ol' Typhoon Johnson up the hill."

"Bah. Typhoon's got more viruses'n a spade full've cats. Ya oughta pay me for drinkin' it."

"You want it or not? On the house."

"Fine."

Simpson turned back to the spaceman. "The difference 'tween our Anchors and IF Anchors is IFs git tuh meet their Anchors. Git pulled right through the Boundary whenever their Anchor calls."

They visit the Real World? the spaceman asked, the awe in his voice evident even through the static crackles.

"That's right. That world you thought you was part of 'til oh-so-not long ago? Them snot-nosed, slick-shit poofs at the table yonder done seen it for real," the cowboy said, pouring the whiskey into his shot glass. He fished out a few wet strings of tobacco and flung them onto the bar floor.

"Makes 'em think they're better'n the rest of us," Simpson said with a hint of venom. "And 'cause they was made perfect, supposably, the ideal specimen fer a real human companion."

"And us, well, we're the supportin' fuckin' cast," spat the cowboy. He fished out another shred of tobacco and flicked it at the table of IFs. It landed about twenty feet short.

If we aren't Imaginary Friends, then... what are we? the spaceman asked. He wondered idly if he'd remember all this tomorrow or if the mind-erasing alcohol would live up to its boast.

"Didn' I jes say?" the cowboy asked. "The supporting fuckin' cast!"

"We're most of us characters in some story er other. Campfire tales, story pamphlets, hell, maybe even movin' pictures, if you believe the stories outta Silver City. Yer 'parently outta some science-fiction, hoodoo nonsense. We here in Gehenna, we're a cowboy tale."

"*The* cowboy tale," the cowboy corrected. "Oldest city in the Bound'ry, Gehenna."

"Aw, hell, you don't believe that shit, G.W."

"Might'n I do," the cowboy said proudly. "Folks was talkin' 'bout Gehenna in the time of the man Jesus, awright. And we's they wayward sinners."

The spaceman settled into himself, deeply troubled. How long had it been since he'd discovered that he was imaginary? Time didn't flow the same in Gehenna; the cowboy was right about that. By his own standards, he would have guessed maybe about a week, but he wouldn't have been surprised to learn it had been a month, either. Or a year. Certainly not longer than that, though? He remembered the details clearly enough. It was Third Lieutenant Pomeroy who'd brought it to his attention in the first place. Where Pomeroy got his intel, God only knew. But Pomeroy pulled him roughly aside during a routine counter-sweep of Jahara's third moon, just before they'd left the outpost airlock. "Listen to me," Pomeroy said, his eyes blazing with fear, or maybe fire. "We can't go out this door."

The spaceman looked at him, confused. "Of course we can. And duty dictates that we shall."

"Fuck duty!" Pomeroy exclaimed in a rare burst of anger. "There's going to be a spontaneous wormhole opening ten yards from here in ten seconds. Anything not bolted down for 100 yards will get sucked back to the Median Era. Including us!" The spaceman remembered the wash of confusion that drenched him there in that airlock. It was the same feeling he had now, sitting at the saloon in Gehenna, trying to comprehend the nature of these IFs. "How can you know that? The very nature of a spontaneous event is that it is unexpected." His first thought, of course, was time travel; Pomeroy had been in contact with a Mover, or maybe he was a Mover himself. But that was ridiculous. Time travel was heavily moderated by the intergalactic governments of both the present and the future, with any sort of deviation from scheduled movements punished severely (often by maiming over death). It was always possible that a Mover had escaped into the pre-time-travel past, then wended his way through to Pomeroy's present to warn him of this impending wormhole. But it wasn't likely. In the first place, the spaceman had heard reliable rumors that timepins were programmed to self-destruct if they were taken beyond the Time Travel Line. And in the second place, Pomeroy was a good soldier and all, but he didn't have any family, and he wasn't exactly the sharpest toolpiece in the rescue kit. It's not like someone would risk intergalactic wrath to travel to a point in Pomeroy's recent past in order to save his life. He wasn't exactly going to forever alter the course of mankind.

But if not time travel, then what? Had Lucas Pomeroy, Third Lieutenant of Bicuspian Platoon, Gamma Sector, gone clinically insane? Such things were known to happen to men who had been in outer space too long. The most popular theory as to why revolved around a scientific breakdown of the various hydrogen compounds that make up the government-regulation Extraterrestrial Replacement Atmosphere (or "plastic air," as it was commonly called among the troops) that made it possible for Earth's space armies to breathe in the deep recesses of the Big Black Vacuum. Speaking for himself, the spaceman suspected it had more to do with the crushing quiet and the inescapable loneliness, along with the ever-present fear of the unknown. But whatever the cause, it was common enough for officers and humps alike to suffer total breakdowns, and that was what he guessed was happening to Third Lieutenant Pomeroy.

"There's been no wormhole activity in this sector for light-miles," he said cautiously, trying to sound soothing. "I'm sure we'll all be f—" But before he could finish the sentence, a wormhole *did* spontaneously appear just ten yards from the outpost entrance – right on the moon's blue, sandy surface – and everything that wasn't bolted down *was* sucked into it (presumably, back to the Median Era), including their rover, an emergency ERA supply tank, the cigarette ash stand just outside the airlock door, and a number of the little five-legged Jahamarans, which had been rooting for planorock before hibernating for the moon's winter. The force of the wormhole even tugged at the solid steel plating of the outpost. The spaceman could hear the structure groan under the strain, but in the end, the building stood strong. And then, several seconds later, with a loud, sucking *POP!*, the wormhole was gone.

The spaceman had turned to Pomeroy, shaking and shaken. "H-h-how did you know that would happen?"

Pomeroy had gripped his shoulders and stared at him with an intensity of understanding. "Because it's happened before."

"What on Earth are you talking about?"

Pomeroy had gone on to explain that he, the spaceman, and every other life form in the universe were no more than figments of some creative's imagination. Pomeroy – Third Lieutenant of Bicuspian Platoon, Gamma Sector, who was a good man but who hadn't the wits to fabricate a white lie, much less an extravagant tale – explained that their lives were on a predestined track and always had been. Their lives and deaths were subject to the whim of a writer, or an orator, or a director, or even a child, for all he knew. They were both imaginary creatures inhabiting an imaginary world, and the worst part of all? Neither of them was the hero of the story. They were casualties, collateral damage, little more than a collective plot point that might create a hurdle for the hero, or relieve a hurdle, or inspire the hero to action. It had happened before, many, many times. But they weren't imagined to remember.

"Nonsense!" the spaceman almost cried. "I have a past! I remember it perfectly! I'm a person, a real human being! You're out of your tree!" All of these things and more, he wanted to say, but then Pomeroy said something that startled him to silence.

"I knew what would happen because it's happened before. We've fallen through that wormhole many times before. Can't you feel it?" And the spaceman was amazed and alarmed to realize that he could. "But this time we've dodged it, and I don't know what will happen now." He paused then, as if waiting for some sort of response from his partner, but the spaceman's throat was choked, and he could say nothing. Pomeroy shrugged his shoulders – an impressively mundane action given the extraordinarily absurd speech he'd just given – and stepped out into the airlock.

The spaceman, in a daze, fumbled with his own helmet and locked it into place before following Pomeroy through the doorway. They passed through the airlock, crossed the surface to the far rover bin, climbed into a spare, and headed back to the ship in silence. Or mostly in silence, anyway. At one point during the drive, Pomeroy pointed to a falling planet blazing in a slow arc high up in the purple sky and noted, with what looked to be a tear in his eye, "We've never seen that before."

They were the last words the spaceman would ever hear him say.

A few kilometers down the path, a heavy wind rushed up around them in the moon's typically calm atmosphere. A gust slammed into the rover so hard, it went up on its right two wheels. The spaceman yelped in surprise. Lime-green bolts of lightning crackled through the air – much closer to the ground than they had any right to be, almost close enough for the astronauts to touch. And in an instant, two new wormholes ripped through the fabric of space, one on either side of the rover. Pomeroy was lifted from the vehicle and sucked into the wormhole on the left; the spaceman clung desperately to the rover, but he was dragged, vehicle and all, into the wormhole on the right.

Which is to say, in the end, the story had its way.

The spaceman felt the odd and painful sensation of being simultaneously flattened and engorged. His body telescoped around and beyond itself, spiraling off into the swirling grayness of the space/time warp. He followed far behind the spiral of his torso for what seemed an eternity. His hands turned to liquid, his feet turned to stone, his lips turned to flames, his bones turned to ice. He screamed in pain and surprise, and the words came out of his mouth. They actually *came out of his mouth* – he could see them spelled out in huge, cartoonish white letters, spinning off behind him as he twisted through the wormhole. His midsection shattered and repaired itself, shattered and repaired itself, shattered again, repaired itself again. The skin dripped from his left hand and exposed his bones, which crumbled into dust and sifted through the air. He blinked, and the hand was restored.

When he was finally pressed through the other end of the wormhole ("pressed" really was the only word he could think of that came close to describing it), he was in a pasture. On what world, he did not know. A herd of sheep was grazing nearby, only they weren't sheep, not exactly. They were short, stumpy-legged things with blood-red fur and bulging eyes, like choking cartoon characters. There were no mouths in their faces; instead, the spaceman saw, they ate through small, tooth-lined openings in their hooves. For some reason, the sight of them unsettled him more than any alien race had before. Never in his life could he even have imagined such an animal.

"Imagined," he said aloud. And so they were. And so was he. And so was Third Lieutenant Pomeroy, and the Bicuspian Platoon, and Mission Control, and everything else he had known in his life. He knew this now, and even though he stood on the far side of the wormhole, dimensions away from everything he'd ever known, he felt an unexplained giddiness. It wasn't just that he found himself on a brand new path; it was that he felt the power to choose which way that path took him. He had shaken off blinders that he hadn't known existed.

Now that the spaceman had been jarred loose of his story, for the first time ever, he was experiencing Free Will.

"You dead in thar?" The cowboy tapped the spaceman's helmet with one lazy, gnarled finger.

No. Sorry. I was just... thinking.

"If yer gonna think, do it some'ere else. It gives me the willies."

You can't possibly know for certain that they're IFs, the spaceman insisted, though he wasn't sure that was right. What was that feeling he'd gotten watching them enter the bar? They gave off that aura, an aura of being... clean? No, that wasn't quite right, but it was probably as close as he could get. There was something entirely too *clean* about them.

"Sure I kin! March yerself over there 'n' check 'em for tags."

Tags? What sort of tags?

"Jesus Hellion Christ, their tags, their tags! Marks 'em as belongin' to an Anchor. Inked on the back o' their necks." The cowboy indicated the spot just above the knob of spine that protruded from between his shoulders. "All IFs're tagged." The spaceman thought about this for a while, and then he made a swift and firm decision. *I want to see.*

He stood up from his stool (not without effort) and hefted his bulky suit around the cowboy, stumbling drunkenly in the direction of the supposed IFs. The cowboy shot out a hand, lightning quick, and grabbed the spaceman's arm. "What the hell're ya doin'?"

I want to see! the spaceman repeated.

"Ya can't jes march over and start pullin' their shirts down. Uncle Moses! Sit back down. Have a little tact." The cowboy put two fingers to his lips and blew out a shrill whistle that cracked through the room. "Hey thar! Yellow hair! C'mere fer a second."

The blond-headed IF looked around uncertainly, trying to determine if he was the "yellow hair" this crazy old man was beckoning, or if it were some other poor fool. "Me?" he finally asked, a practiced smirk on his face.

"Yeah, you. C'mere," the cowboy beckoned with one crooked finger. The blond man whispered something to his companions, and they all laughed. Then he shrugged, pushed his chair back, and joined the cowboy and the spaceman at the bar.

"What's up?"

"Buy you a drink?" the cowboy asked.

The blond man squinted suspiciously. "Sure. I'll have what you're having. Thanks."

"Simpson!"

"I heard 'im." The bartender appeared with an empty, grimy

glass. He swiped the cowboy's bottle and used it to fill the newcomer's glass. The blond man lifted the glass in gratitude, then threw back the shot. The cowboy did the same, and the spaceman poured a trickle of rotgut into his funnel.

"Listen 'ere. Now that we're all friendly, maybe you kin help me settle a bet with my friend, here," said the cowboy. The blond man shifted his pack on his shoulder and inched it around so that the pouch rested at his hip, near his free right hand. "Sure," he said coolly. "What's the bet?"

"My friend the spaceman here bet me twenty pieces that you ain't got a single tattoo on yer body. But I bet he's wrong. Whattaya say?"

The blond man's eyes flashed. His right hand eased to the flap of his pouch. "You trying to start trouble, old man?" he asked through gritted teeth.

"No trouble," the cowboy said, putting on his best innocent eyes. "No trouble at all! Jus' want me my twenty pieces."

The blond man glanced suspiciously at the spaceman, but the golden mirror helmet gave nothing away. He relaxed a bit and let his hand slide back to a comfortable position, away from the bag's flap. "You're out of luck, old man. Sorry." He turned to walk away, but in a flash – faster than either the spaceman or the blond man could have believed – the cowboy whisked his six-shooter out of its holster. He grabbed the blond man by the back of the neck with his left hand and, with a surprising show of strength, whirled him around, slammed him against the bar, and smashed his head down on the oiled wood. The blond man screamed out in pain, but the cowboy put the revolver to his temple and said, "Hush, now. Folks're enjoyin' themselves." At the touch of the cold metal, the IF's mouth stopped moving, though his throat continued to produce mad snarls that matched pace with his heaving chest. The cowboy slid the barrel down the nape of the blond man's neck and pushed the shirt collar down. "See thar," he directed the spaceman. "This'n's got hisself an owner."

The raised, sort-of-black mark stamped into the blond man's nape showed a pair of intersecting circles, one solid, one dotted:

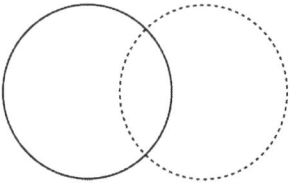

It's more of a brand than a tattoo, the spaceman crackled, rather lamely. But what else could one say in the wake of such a violent unveiling? "Nice ink"?

"This'n's the Anchor," the cowboy said, nudging the solid circle with his pistol barrel, "and this half-in, half-out'n here's fer the IF."

"Let me up, old man," the IF growled into the bar. Tiny flecks of spilled whiskey flew from his lips as he spoke. If he was worried that his friends at the far table weren't rushing over to help him but were instead staring dumbfounded at the old man who'd gotten the drop on their leader, it didn't show in his eyes; they held the cowboy with steel resolve from the corners of their sockets. "You've got three seconds to get your goddamned hands off me."

The spaceman was starting to feel a little nervous; after all, the IF was twice the cowboy's size, half his age, and two and a half bottles more sober. But the cowboy just grinned and gave the spaceman a wink. "Hold them horses, we're jus' 'bout done."

"You're done now." The IF wrenched his arm back and knocked the gun from the cowboy's hand. It went clattering to the floor. Fire flared in his eyes as he flicked open his satchel and drew out a large, finely polished hunting knife. The blade was twice as long as the handle, and the handle was too big for the big IF's hand.

What happened next, the spaceman only saw in quick flicks of time, as if he were looking at still frames from a reel instead of the live-action version. Now the IF kicks the cowboy's chair with one heavy boot; now the cowboy is on the ground, snarling in pain;

now the IF slices with the knife; now the cowboy's hat is on the floor, a long, clean slash in the crown; now the IF holds the knife, blade-down, ready to plunge it into the fallen cowboy; now the six-shooter is in the cowboy's hand. And now the cowboy smiles.

The IF saw the gun, he heard the hammer click, but he was too blinded by rage to care too much. He was the hero in his imaginary world; how in God's name had a weather-beaten, broken-down old cowboy gotten the jump on him? He had been an imaginary friend once, sure, but that was eons ago. The kid who'd conjured him up (Jake, was his name, Jake Nance, a scrawny kid, but good on his feet) was old and grown now, and the IF had made his own way in the Boundary. He was a good man. He was a strong man. He was a fighter. And, if he'd had time to really think it through, he would have seriously doubted that he even could be killed. He was an imaginary person. A figment of some kid's imagination. And if he hadn't kicked off when Jake Nance had graduated high school, he sure as shit wouldn't die now.

But the cowboy's bullets made no distinction between imaginary and real.

The cowboy squeezed the trigger with the self-sure absent-mindedness of a life-long marksman. The IF froze, stunned, as the bullet tore through him: first flesh, then bone, then flesh again. The bar rang with the buzz of the shot. For a long moment, the IF simply stared. But only for a moment.

"My hand!" he shrieked. "You shot my goddamn hand!" He clutched his now crippled right hand with his left and squeezed it to stem the stream of blood pouring out of his palm. The spaceman quietly reached out his right foot, closed it over the hunting knife, which the IF had dropped, and scooted it under his bar stool. No need for this to get any worse than it already was.

Now that their leader was badly, if not exactly mortally, wounded, the other two IFs sprang to action. They jumped from their seats (the pilot took a few hurried pulls from the bottle first) and rushed over to their injured friend. "You people are animals!" the princess shrieked, her eyes wide with horror. She pulled a handkerchief from between her ample bosoms and wrapped it around the adventurer's hand. In seconds, it was soaked through with blood.

"He started it," the cowboy shrugged, putting his stool to rights and grabbing for his bottle.

The pilot grasped the adventurer under the arm and hoisted him onto his shoulder. Together, they drag-hobbled to the batwings. The princess followed close behind, wringing her gloved hands. As the pilot hefted his injured friend through the door, the blond man turned back to the cowboy and shouted, "The Royal's gonna hear about this! You're a dead man! The Royal will see to that! He'll see to you!" And then the trio was out the doors and gone.

Slowly, the bar came back to life. Patrons resumed their conversations, first in hushed whispers, then, gradually, in their regular, jovial tones. Heads swiveled back from the batwings and focused on their drinks, or their card games, or their whores across the table.

Just another night in Gehenna.

The spaceman spun back to the bar, a new (and probably healthy) mixture of fear of and respect for his drinking partner brewing in his gut. He raised a finger, and Simpson brought him a fresh glass. (His original had been shattered during the disruption.) He sipped this one slowly, by way of pouring it into the funnel in little trickles. He screwed up his not inconsiderable brain trying to determine the best way to rekindle a safe conversation, but in the end there was no need. The cowboy spoke first.

"Nice move with the knife," he said, winking conspiratorially. "Yer very own trophy. A memento! Well, one of two."

Two?

The cowboy tapped the spaceman's right arm. The spaceman followed the gnarled finger with his eyes and was shocked to see a shallow tear in the fabric of his spacesuit. "I'm exposed!" the spaceman cried inside his helmet. He grabbed his arm with the other hand and pressed and prodded the sleeve material, examining it frantically for depth. Finally satisfied that only the outer layer of material had been compromised, he let out a deep breath through his exhale vent. He pressed his voice button. *I've never been shot before.*

"Stick 'round, ya'll get another chance," the cowboy grinned. The spaceman frowned.

What did he mean by "The Royal?" the spaceman asked, desperate to change the subject. The cowboy snorted. "Hell, scrat. The Royal's the Top Man. The Big Bull. The Emperor Kiss-His-Assness of the Land."

"Ruler of the Boundary," Simpson added.

"He's a fuckin' dictator," the cowboy said, spitting venom on the floor.

"Careful," Simpson said. He pointed to a rickety, hand-painted sign above the antiquated cash register. It read, LEAKS & POLITICS – TAKE 'EM OUTSIDE.

"Ain' politics," the cowboy insisted. "It's God's honest. Rules by fear. Consorts with demons. Eats the flesh of the livin'." He crossed himself twice and spat on the floor. "Tell me that ain't a fuckin' textbook des-pot."

Simpson rolled his eyes. "I would, if I thought you knew what a textbook was. Where in God's brown earth d'ya pick up this shit?"

"Common knowledge," the older man insisted.

Pardon me, interrupted the spaceman, *and this is just a newcomer's wanting perspective, but your people don't have the look of a people living in fear.*

"That's because we ain't."

"No, it ain't because we ain't, it's 'cause most is gen'rally too stupid to rec'nize it, and also, for those of us with God-gifted smarts, it's 'cause we's too far away from the Pinch to be much concerned."

"We're on the outskirts here. Not as far as the stars, mayhap, but far enough to be left to our own," Simpson explained.

"And it's why I can say the Royal is a blood-suckin', ass-lickin', cock-a-doodlin', no-account, ball-less cock-for!" the cowboy said, more like a petulant child now than the sharp, lethal gunslinger he had been only minutes before.

"Keep it up, and I gotta take ya out," Simpson warned.

The IF spoke as if he had a line to this Royal. Is that likely?

"Gullywash," replied the cowboy. "They's jus' as far from the Pinch as the res' of us, and I'll be toot-damned if the likes've him would design to the likes o' them. What use has the Royal got with IFs? Soft-hand-panderin' sonsovbitches, all of 'em. The Royal don't come from privilege. Prolly hates the IFs more'n anyone else."

"All right," Simpson said, his voice edged with wood. The cowboy's tone had turned sharp, and a few of the other patrons had begun to show signs of unease at the conversation. Generally speaking, too much conversation was bad for business.

But the cowboy went on. "Hell. Fuck do I care if he is cozies with the Grim Reaper? Ol' yellow fuzz kin march back in with the Royal hisself in tow, the nex' bullet goes tween the eyes. Both sets."

Simpson threw his damp rag on the bar in a rare show of frustration. "I think you've had enough fer one night, and I know I have. Pay yer tab 'fore showin' yerself the door."

The cowboy gulped the last three inches of whiskey from his bottle and dismounted the wobbly stool. "Pay ya next Tuesday fer a bottle today," he muttered as he teetered out of the saloon.

Part III: The Surgical Prowess of Those in the Pinch

Simpson lost his grip on the barrel, and the heavy bastard went down on the floor with a dead *THUD*. His heart leapt, fearing for the whiskey inside (and for the money it represented, both in future revenue and in past expenditure), but close inspection of the barrel revealed no leaks, cracks, chips, or splits. He silently blessed Hank Runhill as he wiped the sweat from his brow. A better cooper, there was none.

If you're going to spill that, do it over here, the spaceman said, pointing to his funnel.

Simpson grunted. "Yer startin' to sound like a mutual acquain'nce of ourn."

I suppose someone has to, if said acquaintance is going to maintain this extended absence. Where do you think he's hiding himself?

Simpson shrugged. "Nowheres good, I'd guess." He leaned in close to the spaceman, his eyes wide with concern. "I'll tell ya one thing," he said, his voice low, "that ol' sonofabitch ain't never missed a day at this saloon. Not one single day." He emphasized the point by stubbing his finger against the bar with each syllable. "Not one single day. He's been in here every day of his life, drinkin' my whiskey and offendin' my customers. *Every single day of his life.* You understand what I'm sayin'?"

Yes, yes, he comes in a lot. I understand.

Simpson shook his head. "Not a lot. *Always.* The man don't even have a home. He lives here. He breathes this whiskey. He's the last one out at night, the first one back in the mornin'. That's his role. Ya understand me? That's what he was created fer. To sit at this bar and drink my whiskey and piss people off. But he ain't doin' any of that anymore. And that ain't good."

The spaceman thought on this. *Maybe he found a new bar,* he suggested. Simpson grunted. "Not likely. Ain't in his story, and anyways, ain't no other saloon 'round here fer two-days' ride, and G.W. ain't got no horse." The bartender straightened up and went to work rubbing dirt out of his shot glasses. "Tell ya what, I think we done seen the last o' that cowboy."

As if on cue, the batwing doors creaked open, and the old man himself stepped through the opening. His dirty, floppy hat was pulled down low over his eyes, but it was him, no mistake. Same clothes, same boots, same six-shooter slung low on his hip, same grizzled mustache hanging like twisted, furry icicles from his nose.

Speak of the devil, and he shall appear! the spaceman called. *Welcome back, friend.*

"Where you been hidin' yerself, G.W.?" Simpson asked, a note of joy buried in his ever-stoic tone. But the old cowboy didn't respond. He just shuffled across the floor and made his way to the bar without a word. When he reached it, he just stood there, swaying slightly, like a prizefighter in the fifth round. "G.W.?" the bartender prodded. "Y'alright?"

The cowboy reached into a pocket of his dusty pants and pulled out a fold of money. "I come to pay my bill," he said. His voice was different, somehow; softer and reedy, like a breeze. He set the fold of bills on the bar, then turned on his boot heels and took a step back toward the batwings. The spaceman, who'd been eyeing the cowboy closely, reached out a thickly gloved hand and grabbed the old man by the arm. The cowboy didn't resist, exactly, but he didn't give to the spaceman's force. He just kept walking, pulling his arm along with a surprising strength. The spaceman locked his feet around the legs of his stool, and the cowboy pulled him and the stool across the floor.

Stop! the spaceman cried. *What on Earth has gotten into you?* He leapt off the stool and grabbed at the cowboy with his other hand. This time the old man did put up a fight; in one easy, fluid motion, the cowboy spun and threw a hard left at the spaceman's nose. Or, at least, where he gauged the spaceman's nose to be, concealed as it was under the gold, mirrored helmet. The old knuckles slammed into the surface with a sharp *CRACK*. The spaceman could practically feel the cowboy's joints snapping in the vibration from the helmet. The old man's fingers hung limp, bloodied, and broken from his hand, but the man didn't so much as moan. He just turned and continued on his path toward the doors.

The spaceman, who had let go of the cowboy's arm in surprise, now rushed up behind the old man and bear-hugged him, locking his gloves across the man's chest. The cowboy struggled soundlessly, flailing his boots wildly. He heaved back with a heel, and his gleaming metal spur sliced into the leg of the spaceman's suit. It sliced through the suit's protective layers and buried itself in the spaceman's bare shin. The spaceman howled inside his helmet, his voice agonized and echoing in his own ears. He went down and took the old cowboy with him.

When they hit the ground, the cowboy's hat bounced off his head and rolled toward the doors, as if committed to the escape, with or without its wearer. Simpson, who hadn't touched the stack of bills on the bar, edged around the counter and crept up to the entangled men on the floor. *He gashed my leg!* the spaceman screamed through his speaker. *I'm losing blood! I'm exposed! I'll lose my leg! I'll lose everything!* But Simpson ignored him. There was something else that caught his attention.

He knelt down next to the cowboy, who was still struggling against the spaceman's grip. Simpson pushed the old man's hair back from his forehead. Beneath it, a line of crude leather stitches had been sewn into the cowboy's scalp. The leather string criss-crossed the entire circumference of the old man's head. Blood still oozed from a few of the surgical holes.

"Let him up," Simpson said quietly. The spaceman shouted a string of obscenities, but without his finger on the speaker button, they rattled around inside the helmet and fell on his own ears alone. "Let him go," the bartender said again, gently easing the spaceman's hands apart. The cowboy wriggled free and crawled after his hat.

What are you doing? the spaceman demanded.

"Best to let 'im go. He ain't G.W. no more."

What on Earth is that supposed to mean?

"He's been cleaned," the bartender said sadly. He helped the old cowboy to his feet and watched as the old man swayed out the batwings, never to set foot in the saloon again. "Come on, get up. I'll take ya to the doc."

I demand to know what's going on here! the spaceman said, struggling to his feet.

Simpson shrugged his shoulders, then let them slump sadly at his sides. "You heard him cross the Royal. Looks like the Royal crossed him back." He lifted one finger to his temple and traced a big *X* across it. "That's why we don't talk no politics in this bar."

Later… much later… years later… decades later… the spaceman would have occasion to think back on the cowboy's demise with the absolute empathy that can only come from a shared experience. But for now, he spun slowly back to the bar, and, after wondering his private wonders about the new state of his new friend, he signaled for another bottle of rotgut and flicked open his funnel.

It was just another night in Gehenna.

Pratfall

Benjamin Pippner was not exactly good with mornings. When the alarm went off at 5:30, he half-shuffled, half-stumbled down the creaky wooden stairs and into the kitchen. He hesitated at the light switch, bracing himself for the blast of early-morning blindness. He flipped on the light and, grumbling and moaning, squeezed his eyes shut against the glare. He tripped his way through the kitchen to the far counter and banged and crashed around until he successfully got a pot of coffee brewing in the in the well-worn Bunn-O-Matic. The smell, though pleasant, did nothing to help him shake off the haze of sleep. He would write an angry letter to Folgers that afternoon.

He yawned and stretched, concerned at the inordinate number of cracks and pops, and shuffled his way to the back door. He opened it and squeezed his eyes shut against the sun. Why, why, *why* had he bought a house with a backyard that faced east? He cursed at the sun, which continued to shine undaunted. Then he cursed his paperboy and wished against all hope that he lived on a different route, one controlled by a lad who did not throw the paper over the roof of the house every single morning, like clockwork. It was that stupid boy's fault, he decided, that he had to hiss into the sunlight every morning like some cantankerous vampire. If the paper were in the front yard, it wouldn't be a problem. He apologized to the sun for his harsh words. It continued to shine, still undaunted.

He turned to go back in the house, soggy paper in hand, when something caught the corner of his eye. He whirled back around and saw a short, ratty, violently pale man wearing oversized, worn leather shoes and a frumpy suit coat with a torn bowler hat to match. He looked at Benjamin with sad, wondering eyes. His hands, which had been stuffed inside his dirty pockets, appeared covered in sooty white gloves, and he held them out to the sides and jazzed his fingers, his forlorn expression not changing.

Benjamin turned away from the man, stepped back into his house, and slammed the door shut on his little visitor. Damn hallucinations. They were not entirely uncommon in these wee morning hours. Last week, he saw a tap-dancing panda in the living room. A month before that, it was a smoky-pink genie in the toilet. Leftovers from dreams he could never remember. It took a few slugs of caffeine until his mind sharpened enough to clear them away. This was exactly why he needed to buy one of those fancy-schmancy coffee makers, the ones with the timers that start making coffee while you're still asleep. He couldn't even see straight until he was on his second cup.

The coffee dripped into the pot, and Benjamin grabbed his favorite blue mug from the cabinet. He pulled out the pot and held the mug under the gentle brown stream, both unable and unwilling to wait until the pot was full. Then he replaced the glass pot and let the hot coffee fill him. He looked out the window as he sipped, eyeing the small, pale hallucination in the yard.

"Ben?" The voice of his wife, though rather familiar, startled him. Coffee sloshed over the side of the mug and spilled on his hands. He let a string of curse words fly and shook the coffee from his burned skin. Maggie didn't even seem to notice. She, too, was staring out the window. "Ben, who is that man?"

Benjamin froze mid-shake. She could see him too?
Huh.
Without answering, he retraced his steps to the back door

(stopping along the way to replenish the mug) and stepped out onto the patio. Maggie followed closely behind. They exchanged sideways glances before addressing the vagabond.

"Umm... excuse me," said Benjamin, though he really didn't have to since the man was already looking intently at the pair of them. "Not to sound rude, but... what the hell are you doing in our yard?"

"Benjamin!" his wife chided. "Be nice!"

"Honey, he is clearly a drug-addled homeless man intent on dealing us physical harm!" It was that damn rehab project down the street, he decided. The old, broken-down buildings a few blocks away had been bought by some mega conglomerate or other and were being turned into lofts. The inhabitants of the old buildings – the "squatters" (Ben had another name for them) – had to vacate the premises, and they were now trying to take over the Pippners' backyard by force. But, by God, not without a fight! Ben cursed the conglomerates (which continued to exist, undaunted) and braced himself for early-morning battle.

"Oh, Ben, stop it. He is not," Maggie said. "Excuse me," she called out to the sad stranger. "Can we help you?"

"Maggie!" Ben gasped. "Don't encourage him! Tell him to go away!"

"Stop it!" she hissed. "Act like an adult!" Ben grumped into his coffee. He didn't wanna.

The man's face brightened a little at this show of concern, and he waddled his way closer to the patio. His movements were short and jerky, and yet, exaggerated, almost like a... almost like a...

"Ooooh, no!" said Benjamin, wagging a finger at the approaching hobo. "We do not allow mimes around here, buster!"

"Ben, he is not a mime!" As if in agreement, the little man shook his head and held up his hands in an "empty" gesture. Then he continued to waddle toward the patio, took three steps, tripped over his baggy pants, and tumbled to the ground, finishing in a somersault. He jumped back up, brushed himself off, and made a *ta-da!* show with his hands and face. Ben was not impressed.

"What the hell is this?" he whispered to Maggie. She admitted that she wasn't exactly sure.

"What's your name?" she asked. The man, with a knowing smile, reached behind his back and produced, seemingly from nowhere, a tattered little business card that read *Silent Willy*. "Silent Willy!" chirped Maggie. "Well, isn't that nice!" She leaned over to Benjamin's ear. "Must be a mute," she whispered to him and then turned back to the man. "Well, Silent Willy, it was certainly a pleasure to meet you. I guess we'll be on our way, then!" shouted Maggie, apparently confusing muteness with deafness. With an exaggerated smile, she turned and tried to usher Benjamin and herself into the house.

"Ha!" cried her husband. "You're creeped out by him!"

"I am not!"

"Oh, yes you are! You're trying to give him the brush-off!"

"Well—"

"*Ha!*"

"Oh, shut up," she said, and she took a step toward the house.

Then the music started.

It did not start quietly, no expanding crescendo to ease them in. It blared out, all at once, a rather crude cacophony of horns and drums and crashes and squawks. The Pippners jumped with surprise, but Silent Willy seemed not to notice. He removed a banana very casually from his pocket and began to peel it, slowly and carefully. Benjamin and Maggie watched in utter confusion, their eardrums pulsing with the sound of the invisible orchestra. The little man, having peeled his banana, gobbled it up quickly, then tossed the peel into the yard.

"Hey!" shouted Ben.

The man then stood up and walked away from them, as if to leave. But he slipped on the banana peel. He fell on his back and squirmed his arms and legs in the air for a few seconds before righting himself and standing up straight. He put his hands on his hips and tapped his foot, looking angrily at the banana peel, then picked it up and tried to throw it. But the peel stuck to his hand, and instead of throwing it, he overshot the attempt, and his arm swung violently around in a big circle. The momentum caught him off guard, and he followed the swing of his arm, flipping in a forward circle, once again landing on his back.

Lying on the ground, he tried to shake the sticky banana peel from his hand. It wouldn't budge. He put his hand on the ground and placed a foot over the peel. He pulled. It still wouldn't come loose. He placed his other foot on the peel but missed by an inch and stepped on his fingers. He jumped and made a pained face, but no sound escaped his lips. He hopped around, shaking his injured hand violently, his eyes closed, his mouth formed into a silent O. He didn't watch where he was going, and he crashed into Maggie's favorite rose bush, sticking himself with dozens of thorns. He leapt up at this new pain and darted across the yard, jumping and running in his little jerky, animated motions. The music swelled around them, and as he exited the backyard, a lone trumpet blurted a sad little *waa-waa-waa-waaaah*. And he was gone.

Maggie stared open-mouthed at Benjamin. He just shook his head, sighed, took a sip of his coffee, and headed back into the house. "These silent film stars need to learn a new trade."

Transcript #371

Date: 4/17/2017
Location: Fulton High School Gymnasium
Subject: Mayor John Dooley addressing the citizens of Fulton, Mo. (emergency assembly)
Transcribed by Judy Plantain. Additional notes and emphases by Judy Plantain.

Mayor Dooley:
Good evening, good evening. I'd like to thank you all for making it out to this impromptu meeting on such short notice. I'm glad so many of you were able to come. Now, as your mayor, it is both my duty and my privilege to keep you informed whenever important news occurs in our friendly little town, and I've asked you here tonight because I find myself in possession of just such a bit of news. Now, before I share it with you, it is very, very important that you all promise not to panic. I would like you all to raise your right hands and repeat after me. I, Mayor Dooley.

***Assembly responded.

Mayor Dooley:
No, listen. I say Mayor Dooley, you say your names. Okay? Let's try

again, here we go. I, Mayor Dooley.

***Assembly responded.**
Mayor Dooley:
Do solemnly swear.

***Assembly repeated.**

Mayor Dooley:
Not to panic.

***Assembly repeated.**

Mayor Dooley:
Sir? In the third row, there? Any reason you're not repeating with the rest of the group? If you're set on panicking, sir, I'll need you to leave. Okay? All right, let's continue. I will not panic no matter what sort of bad news I hear.

***Assembly repeated.**

Mayor Dooley:
I will not scream and cause a ruckus.

***Assembly repeated.**

Mayor Dooley:
I will not cry like a little baby.

***Assembly repeated.**

Mayor Dooley:
And I will not try to run away.

***Assembly repeated.

Mayor Dooley:
I understand that if I do panic…

***Assembly repeated.

Mayor Dooley:
…the mayor may put me down with his Taser.

***Mayor Dooley presented his Taser. Assembly repeated.

Mayor Dooley:
Perhaps even unto death.

***Assembly did not repeat.

Mayor Dooley:
Good enough, put your hands down. Now that you've all taken a legally binding oath not to panic—

***District Attorney Blum stood and informed Mayor Dooley that the oath was not legally binding. Mayor Dooley issued an expletive toward District Attorney Blum.

Mayor Dooley:
Now that you've given me your ethically binding word that—

***District Attorney Blum stood and informed Mayor Dooley that the oath was not ethically binding. Mayor Dooley issued an obscene hand gesture.

Mayor Dooley:
--Now that you've given me your ethically binding word that you

will not panic, I have to tell you that the Callaway Nuclear Generating Station has just exploded.

***Assembly responded.

Mayor Dooley:
Please, please! Calm down, remember your ethically binding promise! Now, I know this sounds bad. I mean, it is bad, it's extremely bad. We're not talking a typical nuclear meltdown here, the entire plant has literally exploded, which is much, much worse than a meltdown. Honestly, I've never seen anything like it. Not even in a movie! It's pretty incredible. But please understand, there is absolutely no reason to panic. I spoke with Director Hoffstra at FEMA, and she assured me that they will be able to isolate the contaminated area and seal it off, preventing the further spread of the very potent, very dangerous, and I cannot stress this enough, very deadly airborne nuclear material. But we're well outside the blast radius, so there's really no need to be concerned. The damage has been done, they'll have to turn the entire town of Mokane into a parking lot, and we here in Fulton will carry on as usual. And, hey! Silver lining! We're currently the subject of every major worldwide news feed! It's true, check your phones! We haven't had this much Internet buzz since the plant foreman's three-headed baby got stuck in the well!

*****Mayoral intern Sam Parsons approached the podium and handed Mayor Dooley a notice, which he read silently.**

Mayor Dooley:
Ah. Hmm. Okay. I have just been informed that while we are outside of the blast radius, we are not outside of the contamination radius. Not even close. We're actually, um, wow, actually right smack dab in the center of it. The quarantine includes all of Audrain, Boone, Callaway, Cole, Gasconade, Montgomery, and Osage

Counties. Wow, Sam, even Jeff City? Yes? Ooo, that's bad. So according to this note, FEMA has completely sealed off our borders, and no one is allowed in or out of the city limits. Well, it appears there is a subtle, yet very important difference between the blast radius and the contamination radius, and I…wow, yeah, I totally misunderstood Director Hoffstra's first message. I was like, 'Oh, that's great!' and she was like, 'Huh?' Now that makes sense. Wow, it looks like we are actually not going to be safe. At all. There is a… let's see…some figures scribbled down here…oh, here we go. Yes, okay, there is a 100 percent chance of radiation poisoning for anyone currently within Callaway County limits. That…that doesn't sound promising, does it? Ha, ha. Ooooh boy. Guess that explains the smell in the air, huh? And why my skin is slipping off my hand. Ha, ha. Wow. Yeah, we're all going to die. Well, it could be worse. It could be an election year! Ha, ha. Dodged a bullet! Okay. Well. Tell you what, gang, why don't we all go home and just…wait quietly for death? Sound good? Meeting adjourned.

American Sideshow

Come one, come all, step right up and see the very soul of American entertainment! The bizarre, the macabre, the otherworldly is on the menu tonight!

Come see the aquatic wonder! Half man, half fish, with scales for skin and gills for lungs! A former native of the wondrous Atlantis, now an appetizer for your imagination, and not a bad sight for a measly dollar-fifty, not a bad sight at that!

These acts once entertained presidents and queens! Royalty trilled to the thrills you are about to see! Yes, that's it, step right up, step right up, a small fee is all that stands between you and complete astonishment.

Come ladies, come gents, and see the amazing Miss Zaritha, with a voice to charm the most venomous of snakes! Hips like a river, legs like a fountain, warming the heart of even the coldest-blooded reptiles! If she misses a step, she may take the fangs. (An extra quarter for that one. For her children, you see, and what a deal, no mistake.)

Step up, step up, see the next 10 wonders of the world! Death-defying tricks, gut-wrenching stunts, gruesome gaieties, and an hour's entertainment you won't soon forget, and not a bad price at that, for just a measly dollar-fifty, dollar seventy-five if the snake has his way.

Behind these curtains lives the very essence of America herself! Before there was baseball, before apple pie, the sideshow set the framework for the future of this grand country! Youngsters and oldsters alike gasped and flocked to the sideshow freaks! (Go on in, son, yes, head on in, doniker on the left.)

Yes, in the old days (and the good days, they were), the country teemed with such legendary acts. Traveling circuses made the circuits year after year, enticing the crowds and stealing their hearts. People yearned for the life of the circus gypsy, the unsung hero of the striped big top! Like ranks of proud soldiers, they once populated our lands, but a dying breed is a dying breed, and you can't stop progress, even when progress isn't progress at all, no, ma'am, you can't. Now confined to the heart of Coney Island, you find the last of the great acts: the sword-swallowing sailor, the fire-breathing Balthazaar, the shocking shaman!

How about you, sir? Step right up! See the giants of the stage! (No, sir, not real giants. Lost ours to a thyroid tumor in '87, but the figurative giants are just as good, nay, better!) How about you, ma'am? Come on in, bring the kids, take a gander at the last true sideshow geek. How's that, miss? Yes, indeed, a proud tradition, the sideshow geek. Ain't no act more sideshow than that. Why, you don't know the history of the geek? He bites the heads of chickens clean off, he does, and what a sight that is! (Not to worry, miss, we haven't used real chickens since the suit in '79, just rubber chickens now, just a gag, just a gimmick, just a joke, not even fake blood, no miss, too many complaints, and ain't that the way of it?)

Come on in, ladies and gentlemen, boys and girls, children of all ages! See the amazing pain-proof man, impervious to a thousand rusty nails! See the marvelous elastic woman whose bones are made of pure rubber, I swear it! See the legendary Voltar as we send 10,000 volts through his toes and shoot sparks from his hands!

No, sir, I'm sorry, we no longer offer Jupitra, we just couldn't afford the world's largest woman, she has such a massive appetite, and we only charge a dollar-fifty, you see, and if I may say, not a bad price at that, not for the country's very last ten-in-one.

Oh? You say you might be back? Yes, ma'am, show every hour on the hour. Come on back, and I'll hold you to it. Can't beat the price, after all, just a measly fee.

Just a dollar-fifty (dollar seventy-five if the snake is extra-charming), can't beat that price, not nowhere these days, not no how. Price the same now as it was in '71. Inflation, it goes up, but the price of thrills, that stays the same. A mere pittance now… we could charge twice the amount – no, three times the amount! – but we'll keep it low for you. Yes, sir, inflation goes up, but the price of a dying livelihood stays the same. Genocide comes cheap, isn't that what they say? Ha ha, no, of course not, sir, just a joke, just a joke, everything here is for show. Won't you step inside?

If good, clean fun just ain't your thing, I know what that ilk needs, and ain't we got somethin' for it! Come on back for the burlesque show, starts at quarter of nine (now that's the real money-maker), five dollars a head, and worth every penny, worth twice the price! 18 and over, no children allowed, the burlesque can fulfill your desires, all right. You'd pay ten times as much for the same sights in Manhattan, maybe twenty. One show a night, and make no mistake, worth every penny at least.

Step on up, step right up, the show's about to start! Darling Daisy, the sword-swallowing starlet! Gums McKinsey, the glass-eating wonder! We can sing, we can dance, we can laugh, we can cry, we can scare, we can thrill, we can live, we can die. Step inside the curtain, the show's about to start!

Step up, step up, see the death of America! Available to you for just a handful of dimes! It's Custer's slaughter, it's Kennedy's last ride, it's Hemingway's mouth on the barrel! It's great and pure and real and American and laid to waste by the flame of time! Just a dollar-fifty to strike the match!

Where are you going? The show's about to start! We've mutilated ourselves for sideshow art! Haven't you ever believed in something that strongly? Haven't you fought in a battle that's already been lost? Don't you know the high price of faith?

We do. It's a dollar-fifty. Dollar seventy-five if the snake gets restless. And at that price, it's a steal.

Come all.

Or come one.

Don't you want to see the show?

The Rapture and Charlie Gumphrey

If there were one thing to be said for Charlie Gumphrey, it was that he was ready for the rapture. Some men had a knack for business. Some excelled at sports. Charlie Gumphrey was a world-class rapture anticipator. And that's just the way it was.

His fellow non-denominational Christians might ask him, "Charlie, when do you think the rapture is likely to occur?" And Charlie certainly answered, "Why, at night, of course! For when the Lord returns in his fiery glory, the flames will best be viewed against the darkness."

"Charlie, will the rapture occur during our lifetimes?" they would ask. "Oh, absolutely," Charlie said. "For the human race is as desperate now as it is ever likely to be!"

"And Charlie, who will be saved?" they would further inquire. "Why, certainly me," he responded, "and hopefully you!"

Of course, it was one thing to speak intelligently (and, daresay, prophetically) about the Second Coming, but it was quite another thing indeed to live in a perpetual state of preparedness. That's why Charlie always slept in very modest pajamas, lest the Lord should see him in something a little skimpier upon His return and question the man's worthiness. Of course, his clothes would be left behind when the rapture was finally enacted, but only after Charlie had transitioned to his Heavenly body. During those first crucial minutes when the actual judgment occurred, Charlie wanted to be sure he was properly covered.

It is also why, as a general rule, he kept his earthly debts quite up to date. He certainly did not want to have poor credit to report when Jesus came to collect the faithful, for how would that look to the Almighty? "Here stands a man full of faith, but empty of sound economic sense," the Lord might say, and that would never do, because all good Christians are in Heaven's debt, and the Almighty must be assured that it can be paid back. The First Bank of the Second Coming, that's where we'll balance our eternal deficit, and as the prayer says, on Earth as it is in Heaven! Besides, Charlie knew that not everyone would be assumed into Heaven when the final judgment took place, and he suspected that credit card companies might still be operating with a full staff the morning after the rapture. But once he was no longer a part of this world, he couldn't possibly be expected to keep making monthly payments. As he had no children to inherit his bills, he knew he would no doubt be publicly wracked and slandered by collectors before his clothes finished fluttering to the floor, and he simply refused to allow even these most devious of sinners the opportunity to speak ill of him once he'd been saved.

He also kept a note taped to his headboard that would explain everything to his landlady once he disappeared. It gave all the details of the rapture, at least insofar as he felt comfortable describing in his own mortal words. He described the event – what it meant, why he had been chosen, why she hadn't been, and so forth. In a postscript, he also asked her to feed his cat, John the Baptist, just in case felines weren't included in God's final plan. Admittedly, he really wasn't sure if animals would be assumed or not, and he wanted to provide for his poor little tabby if worse came to worst. The note also provided instructions on what to do with his belongings. Under normal circumstances, of course, he would have donated everything to the poor, for he was a dutiful, generous Christian. However, in the event of the rapture, all worthy recipients would be gone from this earth, and as only the heathen hordes would be left to claim his charity, he ordered all of his belongings to be burned to cinders.

Although he owned a car, he only drove it in emergency situations, because he did not want to be responsible for the deaths of any of those left behind (heathens though they might be) when he disappeared from behind the wheel and sent the machine careening Lord knows where and crushing Lord knows whom. Again, he was as certain as he could be that the rapture would occur at night when he was home in bed, but you can't be too careful about these sorts of things, and, as any good Christian will tell you, it never pays to gamble.

Every night, Charlie slept with a flashlight clutched tightly in his hand, in case he needed one in Heaven. He suspected that God's Paradise would be adequately lit, but he wasn't so sure about the actual assumption. The only way to Heaven was up, up, up, past God only knows how many miles of space, and space was dark. He didn't need to see where he was going, of course; he knew God would guide the worthy. And he wasn't even sure he'd be able to bring the flashlight with him, as it might have to remain in his room with his sensible pajamas. But Charlie anticipated the Pearly Gates so strongly that he allowed himself the hope that he might be able to spy them before anyone else if he only had a light to shine on them from a great spatial and dimensional distance. He'd waited his whole life to see those gates; he wouldn't want to wait any longer than was absolutely necessary. (Yes, it's true. This could be construed as a vanity of sorts, but Charlie allowed himself this one tiny breach, for he felt he'd earned it by living his life as stalwartly as he did.)

All these preparations were second nature to Charlie, who had been waiting for the rapture since childhood. He refused to end up like the doltish bridesmaids of biblical fame, caught off guard when the bridegroom Jesus appeared at His metaphorical wedding. That would be foolishness itself. So every night, when he said his prayers, he patiently asked God to let the rapture come soon, for he was ready to come home.

One night, Charlie was woken quite abruptly from his sleep by a noise from the front hall. Was it a burglar, come to indulge his sinful cravings with Charlie's mortal goods? Or – hope against hope and dream against dream! – was it the Second Coming, at long last, after all his careful planning and long, long waiting? But no, Charlie realized with a sudden heaviness of heart, it couldn't be that, for he was still dressed in his very modest pajamas, and there were no fires of judgment blazing in the skies.

But it wasn't a burglar, either. It was a visitor, a visitor knocking gently but urgently on the front door. That was the sound that had awoken him from his slumber! Charlie looked at the alarm clock next to his bed. 3:16 a.m. Who on earth could it be?

He flicked on his flashlight and stumbled drowsily into the front hall. Whoever was on the other side seemed extremely anxious to be let in. The knocking became less gentle and gave way to rapid pounding. Charlie put his eye to the peephole. "Who is it?" he asked through a yawn. But as he beheld the distorted fish-eye view of his guest, he already knew who it was. He knew by the glittering white robe and the well-trimmed brown beard.

It was Jesus.

"Girl Scouts, I have your cookies. No, just kidding. It's Jesus. Can I come in?"

Charlie swooned and nearly cracked his head on the doorknob. He simply couldn't believe it! Could it be? A non-rapturous visit from the Lord? What an honor! He steadied himself against the jamb and set his trembling fingers to work on the lock. "Just a second!" he called. *Just a second?* What a maroon! Who tells Jesus that he'll be with him in just a second? Oh, pitiable Charlie Gumphrey, whose drowsiness has become his demise!

"Sorry, Lord!" he cried out, fumbling with the latch. His fingers finally did their duty, and the bolt slipped back. Charlie yanked open the door. "Hello, sir!" he shouted nervously. "Please, please, come in!"

"Hey, thanks." Jesus sauntered into the foyer, and suddenly the entire apartment was flooded with bright, dazzling whiteness. Not light, per se. Just… whiteness. *And so my apartment is washed clean in the blood of the Lamb,* Charlie thought. Jesus chuckled. "Ha ha! Totally."

Charlie closed the door and ushered Jesus in. The Son of Man tipped his head graciously and headed for the living room. "Cool if we chat in here, Charlie?" He asked.

"You know my name!" he exclaimed, rather stupidly.

Jesus flopped down on Charlie's one couch and sat back, crossing his legs. "Yeah, well, you know," He said, pointing to Himself with the index fingers of both hands. "Jesus."

"Of course. Right. Of course you know my name. I'm sorry, I—would you like some coffee?" Was he making a bad first impression? He didn't want Jesus to think him a simpleton. He was just too stunned to think clearly, and too sleepy, that was all.

"Nah, thanks, Charlie. I'm good. I grabbed a Red Bull on my way down."

"Really?"

"No, just kidding. That stuff's awful for you. Gives you this energy high, then you crash hard. Hard enough you're not going to rise three days later, know what I'm saying? Ha, ha!"

"Oh." Charlie perched on the edge of the armchair and smoothed his nightshirt. Even if he was making a bad impression, at least he was wearing modest pajamas. Score one for preparation. "You know, Jesus, You look exactly like I always pictured. I mean, with the beard, and the robe, and, gosh, I was in New York City this one time—I know, I know, test of faith much?—and I heard this man shouting in an alleyway, and he was talking about You and said You were really a darker-skinned person, but I knew You were white like the rest of us, I just knew it."

"Hm?" said Jesus absently. He looked down at himself. "Oh, right. Yeah. I toned it down for you. I'm glad you like it. So listen, Charlie, I can't stay long, but I came to talk to you about—ooo, hey, are those Fritos?" He had noticed a rumpled bag of them on the end table. Charlie cursed himself silently for leaving such a mess out in the open. Cleanliness, after all, is next to godliness. But Jesus waved off his self-reproaching thoughts. "Oh man, chili cheese! Those are the best. Do you mind?"

Charlie wagged his head. "No! No, by all means! Help yourself!"

"Awesome. Thanks." Jesus retrieved the bag and brought it over to the couch. He munched as he talked. "You know, you humans do some pretty screwy things sometimes, but man, Fritos are great! Boffo!" He licked chili-cheese-flavored dust from his fingers. "But that's not what I'm here to talk about. Look, Charlie, I just dropped by to tell you, you've got this rapture thing all wrong." Charlie's heart sank into his stomach. He suddenly felt like he was spinning down an extraordinarily long hole.

"All wrong? What do you mean all wrong?" He had spent his whole life believing and preparing, ever since he was a small boy. How could it possibly be wrong? "I mean, hear Me out," Jesus continued. "You've done a good job here, keeping yourself ready for the Second Coming and all, and you're a good guy! Don't think that's gone unnoticed. The thing is, you've just got the wrong idea. This whole 'rapture' thing, it's not really Me, you know? I mean, it's quick, it's to the point, and I like that. It's got dramatic flair. Everyone loves a little theatre, am I right?" He waved his hands in front of his face, and a bright spark like a firecracker exploded between his palms. "Bang! Ha, ha! Love that." Charlie nodded sickly. "But, I don't know, I'm picturing something a little more… a little more subtle, you know? A little more open and loving. Seems pretty harsh to just leave a few hundred million people behind without any explanation, you know? 'Hey, nice try, buuuuuuut you're doomed.' Pretty brutal, no?" He craned his neck to look around the corner at the refrigerator. He clicked his tongue in disappointment. "No chocolate milk, huh? That's a shame. These things go great with chocolate milk."

Charlie dropped his forehead into his open, shaking hands. How could this be? How could this possibly be? All his careful preparations… all his preaching and testifying… was all of that really for naught? Had he wasted his entire life planning for a fiery judgment that wouldn't come?

"So that's a solid no on the chocolate milk, then?" Jesus asked a little awkwardly. "You don't have, like, a basement fridge or something?"

"Hm? Oh. No. Sorry," he said, his small voice barely more than a whisper. "I don't like to keep things that might spoil. You know. For when the—" He couldn't bring himself to say it.

"The rapture, right, sure, got it. That makes sense. Well, no worries. I'll grab some on my way out. I saw a 7-11 around the corner." He propped Himself back against the couch, tilting the Fritos bag so the last few crumbs tumbled into His mouth. "Look, Charlie," He said, chewing, "you seem pretty upset about this whole thing. I don't want you to take it personally, all right? By no means is this a reflection on you. You're doing what you think is right, and hey, can't ask for more than that, huh? I'm just saying, maybe you should spend a little more time living your life, you know? Don't spend every waking hour making sure you're ready to move onto the next life. I mean, anticipate it and everything – do good works here for the Kingdom and all that – but enjoy this life while you've got it. It's a gift, you know?"

Charlie nodded miserably. What a night, what a night! He should have stayed in bed. Here he was, with Jesus Christ sitting in his living room, and it should be the happiest, greatest moment of his existence. But instead he was being lectured to. And don't take it personally? How could he not take it personally? Jesus had come to him, personally, to tell him how wrong he was! How was that not personal?

Unless… unless… of course! Charlie thought, brightening instantly. This was a test! It had to be! Right? The Lord was testing him to make sure he was really a believer! What a sly trick! Well,

Charlie would show Him, all right! He wouldn't just cast his beliefs aside like some doubting Thomas! He'd keep on preaching the rapture until Kingdom come! He would prove his—

"No, Charlie, listen," said Jesus, standing up and stretching. "It's not a test. I'm just trying to tell you, when the end times do come, they're going to be a little… softer. Oka?" Charlie stared quietly at the Lord, his lip quivering. Jesus checked his watch. "Hey, listen, I have to run. There's this building in Singapore, it's going to collapse if I don't get out there, so…" He picked up the empty bag of Fritos and tossed it into the waste bin in the hall. He plucked a washcloth off the shelf from inside the bathroom, dampened it in the sink, and wiped the Fritos dust from his mouth and beard. "But think about what I said. Keep living a good life, Charlie, but really live it, okay? You only get the one shot down here. Trust me, the final reward comes soon enough." He walked to the front door and pulled it open with no trouble from the bolt whatsoever, even though Charlie was sure he'd locked it behind him. Jesus turned back to look at his host, who had not moved a single muscle in the last minute or so and who looked quite like a sick fish. "I love you, Charlie. Keep fighting the good fight." He pumped a fist in the air, held it there for a second, and then, in a whirl of robes and light, He was gone.

Charlie didn't move. He couldn't move. The whole episode had happened as if in a dream, but of course it was not a dream. The washcloth in the bathroom was proof enough of that. When Jesus had patted his face with it, His image had transferred, leaving a two-dimensional, 100% cotton reminder of His visit.

Charlie sat perched on his armchair until the sun crept over the horizon and light began to filter into the apartment. He was dumbfounded; that was the only word for it. He had found dumbness. He suspected he was numbfounded as well, for it wasn't just his voice that didn't show any signs of life. It was his whole being.

To put it quite mildly, Charlie was wracked with confusion. The rapture was real. It was *real*. It had to be. Not just because he'd prepared for it his entire life, but because every trusted spiritual advisor he'd ever known had said so. The mass of the faithful had assured him again and again and again. But here, the Lord had given him straight advice, and wasn't He infallible?

Live a life? Forget the judgment? Expect something softer? Don't be in a hurry? Could these really be the directives of the strong and vengeful God who had awed him since birth?

It was a deep, difficult struggle for Charlie, and he spent days – no, weeks – worrying his own heart and agonizing over his course of action. But finally, finally, after countless hours of soul searching and personal reflection, Charlie Gumphrey made a decision, and in the end, he did what any true believer would do when so apodictically confronted with his own grievous misunderstanding of the Divine Plan.

Charlie Gumphrey became agnostic.

The Sandalman Song

The seven children clasped their little hands and spun around together in a little circle. They sang their favorite little song:
Beware, beware, of the Sandalman twins.
The terrible two make you pay for your sins.
One lies in dreams, one lies awake,
Better say you're sorry, for goodness sake!
Brother chews your fingers up to taste the blood,
Sister bites your toes off and sucks on the mud.
Once they come to bed, they won't leave 'til they're through,
Mommy and Daddy will forever miss you!

When the song finished, the children unclasped their hands (as they always did), threw them into the air (as they always did), and fell backward into the grass, screaming and wiggling their hands and feet, just as they always did. Oh, the Sandalman song was their favorite game! This last part, when you fell into the grass, was the very best because that was when you pretended like Brother Sandalman was chewing up your fingers and Sister Sandalman was biting up your toes! What fun! The children giggled and wiggled their fingers under each other's noses. Little Jimmy was the first to say, "My fingers are all chewed up!" And all the other children laughed. Little Missy was the first to shout, "My toes are all bitten off!" And all the other little children laughed even harder.

But one child did not laugh very hard. In fact, one child did not laugh at all. You see, Little Freddy was new to the neighborhood and had never heard the song before, and he didn't know that when you finished the song, you were supposed to fall into the grass and wiggle your fingers and toes and pretend they were being gobbled up by the Sandalman twins. How could he know? The other children had lived in the town their entire lives, and they had grown up with the song. But not Little Freddy. He felt embarrassed for not knowing how to play, and he told Little Suzie so, but Little Suzie just laughed and said he shouldn't be embarrassed at all.

"Our parents don't like it when we play," she confided between giggles, "but it's our favorite! I'll teach you!"

But Little Freddy did not think it would ever be his favorite game. He didn't dislike it, exactly, but he didn't much like it, either. Something about the words made him feel, well, *afraid*, if he were being honest with himself. He decided to tell that to Little Suzie, too.

"Oh, Freddy," said Little Suzie, as she stood up from the ground and brushed the grass off her dress. "It's just a game."

Just then, someone – Little Jimmy, maybe, or perhaps Little Tommy – said, "I can hear the ice cream truck!" And the other children listened very, very hard, and then they could hear the ice cream truck, too! They ran around the block to catch up to the truck, which was very far away.

But Little Freddy did not run after the ice cream truck. He was still troubled by the Sandalman song. "I've never heard another song quite like that one," he said to himself. "I think I want to know more about it." He wished (and not for the first time) that he were still back in his old town and not in this new town, because he knew exactly where the library was in his old town, but he did not know where the library was in this new town. He did not like this new town. He thought that it felt... wrong.

Well, he would have to do some detective work to find the library, if the town even had one. In the meantime, Little Freddy decided that he would ask his parents if they knew about the Sandalman song. He set off for home.

It was almost dark when he got there. He expected his mother and father to be upset with him for being out so late, but instead they hardly seemed to notice that he had returned, or that he had even been gone in the first place. They were sitting at the kitchen table when he entered the house, not really doing anything, just sitting quietly. They weren't even looking at each other. They didn't look up when he slammed the door. They didn't respond when he said hello.

They had been like that a lot, lately. Ever since the move. They didn't speak to him much anymore. They didn't hug him much anymore. They didn't *notice* him much anymore, really. Little Freddy was very troubled by the way his parents were acting, and he forgot to ask them about the Sandalman song. Instead, he decided he would just get ready for bed. Maybe his mother would come tuck him in. Maybe she wouldn't.

Little Freddy changed into his favorite blue pajamas and brushed his teeth and said his prayers as he climbed into bed. *Bless Mommy and Daddy and make us okay*. He called out to his mother and father to tell them he was going to bed now – even though it was quite a bit earlier than his normal bedtime – but they did not answer. He pictured them in his mind, still sitting at the kitchen table, not moving, not speaking. Just sitting. He didn't like thinking about that, and he wished they would come in to say goodnight.

But they didn't.

Little Freddy worried himself about his parents as he lay in bed. He worried so much that he almost didn't remember about the Sandalman song before he fell asleep. Almost. As he drifted off to dreams, the last little part of the song played in his mind, and he could hear the voices of the other children singing it, even though they sounded far away.

Once they come to bed, they won't leave until they're through,
Mommy and Daddy will forever miss you.

Little Freddy started having a strange dream. He dreamt that he was back with the other children, his new little friends, and they were all forming a circle, just like they had earlier that day, but this time, Little Freddy was not part of the circle. He was in the center, and the other children circled around him, their hands clasped, their lips flying in little whispers. Something else was different, too. The other children didn't really look like children. Not exactly. Their skin was ashen; their cheeks sunken and pinched. Some of them had holes where their cheeks should be, and Little Freddy could see their teeth working through their skin. The children's hair was all long and dirty, like they had been swimming in a swamp or dragged through the woods. But they were all smiling, just like they always did. Even so, Little Freddy was just a little bit afraid of them. When he really thought about it, they didn't look much like his new friends at all.

They were all singing the Sandalman song, too.

Beware, beware, of the Sandalman twins. The terrible two will make you pay for your sins.

The children spun around Little Freddy, faster and faster, until they were a blur, and in the blur, Little Freddy saw something that scared him, scared him very much. He saw that one of the little children was not a little child at all, but an old woman, very thin and frail, but still taller than the children and filthier. She was moving in the circle, too, but unlike the children who were whirling, twirling blurs, he could see the dirty old woman very clearly as she circled him, and she was staring right at him – right *into* him, if that made any sense. Her eyes were all black, almost like they weren't eyes at all but shiny, glistening sockets. She smiled, too, just like the little children, but her teeth were sharp and pointy and mostly yellow with little pink stains on them.

Little Freddy didn't like that woman at all.

One lies in dreams, one lies awake, better say you're sorry, for goodness sake!

She wasn't singing like the other little children were. She wasn't laughing, either. She was only smiling her dangerous smile. And she was licking her teeth, and since they were so very sharp, she cut her tongue on them every time she licked. Blood dropped onto her lips, but she kept doing it anyway. Her shiny black eyes stared right at Little Freddy.

Brother chews your fingers up to taste the blood, Sister bites your toes off and sucks on the mud.

The little children kept singing. Even though they were right next to him, their voices sounded so far, far away. And still they spun, faster and faster. They spun so fast that little, tiny pieces of them began to fly off. Little, tiny pieces of skin and little, tiny pieces of teeth and little, tiny pieces of hair pitched into the air. Some of the pieces landed near Little Freddy, others landed on Little Freddy. But the children didn't seem to notice. They still spun very, very quickly.

Once they come to bed, they won't leave 'til they're through,
Mommy and Daddy will forever miss you.

The children threw up their hands and fell onto the ground laughing, just like Little Freddy knew they would. But when they hit the ground in this dream, some of their limbs crumbled off, like they were rotted through. Little Missy's arm crumbled off at the shoulder. One of Little Jimmy's eyes rolled right out of its socket. This was extremely disturbing for Little Freddy, but even more disturbing was the fact that the sharp-toothed woman had not fallen to the ground like all of the little children. She was still standing, and she was still smiling. She was still licking her teeth, and she was still looking right at Little Freddy.

"No!" Little Freddy screamed. "Wake up!" And he did. He woke up in his own bed, in his room, and he was sweating. The covers twisted around his ankles, pinning him to the sheets, but he was awake, and the decaying children and the blood-toothed old woman were gone. Little Freddy cried then, cried for the first time in years, and he covered his head with the blanket.

But something tried to pull it back down.

Little Freddy couldn't see what was tugging at the blanket. It was dark as a cave under the cover, and whatever was pulling at it was on the outside of the blanket anyway. He could feel something grabbing the blanket right near his head and pulling down, hard. Little Freddy was sure he was not dreaming, but he was also sure that whatever was pulling at the blanket was neither his mother nor his father. He knew that because whatever was pulling at the blanket smelled like rotted mushrooms, and neither of his parents smelled like that.

Little Freddy was so very frightened. He squeezed his eyes shut and held the blanket tightly over his head. The thing tugging the blanket tugged harder, and Little Freddy held tighter. He could hear the thing on the other side of the blanket panting, its hot, sour breath warming the cotton pressing against his nose. Little Freddy wanted very much to scream to his parents, but when he tried, no sound came out, and even if he were able to scream, he did not think they would come help him. They were so uninterested in him lately, ever since the move to this new town.

So instead, Little Freddy tried hard to ignore the thing that was trying to pull back his blanket, and he tried to force himself back to sleep. If he could go to sleep, perhaps he could have a good dream instead of a bad dream, and then he wouldn't even notice that he was sleeping at all, and he would sleep through the whole night, and when he woke up in the morning, the thing that was pulling at his blanket would not be there anymore, and he would be safe. Besides, Little Freddy was very tired, much more tired than he usually was, and he was able to fall into a light sleep, even though the sour-breathed something was pulling at his covers and scaring him very much.

Little Freddy *did* have a dream when he fell back to sleep, but it was not a good dream. In fact, it was the same dream he had before. He was in the middle of the ring of little children, and they were running around him in a blur and singing the Sandalman song, which was their most favorite game. But there was one thing different this time, and the one thing different was that the old woman was not in the ring of children. He looked wildly around the circle but did not see her. He felt a little bit relieved by that; perhaps this dream was different after all. The other children still looked not much like themselves, and their limbs were still rotted and tearing apart, and they still scared him a little, but the old woman was the scariest of all, and he was so happy that she was no longer in the circle.

Then something tickled at Little Freddy's toes, and he realized that in his dream he was barefoot. This was strange for Little Freddy, because he so very rarely went anywhere without socks and shoes. You never knew what sort of rough terrain you might find yourself in over the course of a day, or what germs you might have to slosh through at any given time. The tickling at his toes bothered him, and he looked down to see what it was that was tickling him so, and when he did, he lost his breath, like someone had punched him in the stomach, because the old woman had not gone away after all. She was on the ground, at his feet, and she was licking at his toes with her tongue, which was still just a little bit bloody, and she looked up at him with her wet, black eyes, and she smiled a wicked smile. Then she lowered her dirty, pinched face down to his bare feet and sunk her sharp, jagged teeth into his toes.

Little Freddy cried out in pain, and he screamed for help, but the other children ignored him; they were so busy playing their most favorite game and singing their most favorite song. The old woman chewed at his toes, sucking the dirt and the mud and the blood, just like the song said, and oh, Little Freddy was in so much pain, and he wanted so badly to wake up. He squeezed his eyes shut and screamed inside his head, and then he awoke, finding himself once again in his own bed with the covers pulled up over his head.

Except that wasn't quite right. The covers were *not* over his head. The covers had been pulled down. Because his head was no longer hidden by the blanket, he could see the thing that had been pulling so very hard at his covers, and what he saw froze his blood in his heart so much that his chest might explode into a million tiny ice crystals. Because the thing that had pulled his blanket down looked very much like the old woman from his dream, except that this thing (who was really a person, Little Freddy supposed) was bigger and had shorter hair and was not an old woman, but an old man. And then Little Freddy knew who the old man was, and he knew who the old woman was, too. They were Brother and Sister Sandalman, and they were twins.

Brother Sandalman smiled down at Little Freddy with the same sharp, wicked smile as Sister Sandalman. Little Freddy, numb though he was, realized that the old man held something in his hands. The something the old man held was Little Freddy's hands. Little Freddy tried to pull them back, but Brother Sandalman held them tightly in his cold, slimy grip, and he was very strong. This time, Little Freddy did scream for help, because he knew he was awake, and he could not escape from Brother Sandalman, because he was so very real. But even though he screamed loudly – loudly enough to rattle the toys inside the boxes he hadn't yet unpacked – his parents did not come to help him, as if they didn't hear him, or as if they didn't care.

Little Freddy was too frightened to notice that even though he was awake, his toes really had all been chewed up.

Brother Sandalman brought Little Freddy's fingers to his mouth and started nibbling at them with his sharp, jagged teeth. The wrinkled old demon mumbled angrily as he chewed, and his wet, clumping hair brushed and clung to Little Freddy's wrists. Each time Brother Sandalman sank his teeth into a smooth, narrow piece of flesh, Little Freddy cried out in pain and terror. In no time at all, Brother Sandalman was down to the second knuckle. The pain and the fear were so great that Little Freddy fainted.

And when he fainted, he started to dream again…

The next morning, Little Freddy's parents decided to move away from their new home. They decided they did not like this new town, and they could not precisely remember why they'd moved here in the first place. They wished they had never come here, though they could not exactly say why. This new town made them a little sad. Perhaps it was because they saw so many children playing in the neighborhood, and this made them long for a child of their own. They had never had a child of their own, you see, and they were so very lonely.

And after they moved, the house stood empty for a time, but not for too long of a time; soon, a happy new family looked at the house and thought that perhaps they would like to buy it and live there. They were such a happy little family indeed – a mother, and a father, and a son, a little boy named Billy. The mother and the father thought that this town would be a wonderful place to raise Little Billy, because the town was full of so many happy children. They thought that Little Billy could play with the little children. Perhaps they would let him play their most favorite game. They could even hear the children singing their favorite song from somewhere down the street, even though it sounded so very far away. The mother and the father did not know the song, but they thought it sounded like fun, and they hoped that Little Billy would learn it, too.

And when all the children met Little Billy, they were so happy to teach him the song. It was their most favorite game.

Clarence

Clarence was not a camel. He was an accountant. This is an important distinction to make. It is precisely why the following events are so baffling.

It all started one morning in early March. Clarence, a quiet man known to his co-workers as an unassuming gentleman of rather strict habits, arrived at the office clad in a sleek new sport coat. Now, on any other man, such a paltry change in attire might not have caused much commotion, or perhaps any commotion at all. Clarence, however, was not just any other man. He had worn one of two jackets to work every day for the entirety of his career at Bateman-Wayne, a career that spanned more than 15 years. Clarence was a simple man, and he hadn't much cause for more than two sport coats. Needless to say, it was quite a shock to the surrounding cubicle community when he showed up that particular morning in a new dark-brown jacket.

Although everyone on Clarence's floor noticed the jacket, Ronnie the mail boy was the first to actually comment on it. "Yo, Clare!" he said through the blare of rock music from his headphones. "Sweet coat, man. Real leather?"

Clarence, who had been sitting very peaceably working on the Beaumeyer account, looked up with a rather pained expression on his face. "Why, no," he said, sounding a bit surprised. "Not at all. It's camel hair."

"Camel. Rock on, man. Camels are flippin' sweet." And Ronnie was off to deliver mail to the next row. But the damage had been done. Roger Swinton peeked his head over the wall that separated his workstation from Clarence's.

"Hey, Clarence," he said. He had not spoken to Clarence more than four times in the twelve years they had been neighbors. "Did I hear that right? Camel hair?"

Clarence stroked his left sleeve absently. "Of course," he replied. "What else?"

"I don't know." Roger shrugged. "I didn't know they made camel-hair jackets anymore."

Clarence looked frightfully confused. His face twisted in an uncertain grimace. "There are always camels," he said. "There must always be camels."

Roger shrugged again. "I guess that's true. I don't know. I've never been to Africa." And he sunk back down into his cubicle.

Yes, Africa, Clarence thought. *Hmm. Africa...*

Later that morning, Clarence marched into the cushy corner office of the district manager, Walton P. Cunnyweather. He, Clarence, was chewing violently on what must have been a piece of gum the size of a softball. "Mr. Cunnyweather," he said between lip smacks, "do you have a moment?" Cunnyweather, who had nothing but spare moments, furrowed his brow quite intensely.

"I'm very busy, Clarence," he lied. "Extremely busy. What do you need?"

"Well," said Clarence, chewing viciously, "I've been wondering about—"

"Clarence," Cunnyweather squirmed, "must you smack your gum about in my presence? Really, it's enough to make me toss my lunch."

"Gum, sir?" Clarence asked with a frown. "I'm not chewing any gum, sir."

"Oh, really?" asked Cunnyweather as he leaned back in his

swivel chair, not to be made a fool of. "Then what, may I ask, are you chewing?" Clarence gaped at him like he was the biggest dolt on the planet.

"Cud, sir," he said. "Obviously."

Cunnyweather physically shook off this ridiculous comment. "Look, what do you want?"

"I was wondering about our corporate frequent flyer miles," said Clarence.

"Yes? What about them?"

"Well, they only go to certain places, right?"

Cunnyweather was beginning to feel uneasy. The insane chewing was really getting to be a bit much. "Yes, yes. So?"

"Well, sir, I was wondering," said Clarence. "Do they go to Africa?"

Cunnyweather stopped avoiding eye contact with Clarence. He studied the man's face for a bit, searching for a sign of tomfoolery. He found none. "Why on earth would you want to go to Africa?" he asked.

"It's a well-documented fact that it's where camels belong, sir."

Cunnyweather twisted his head at Clarence. "What the devil does that have to do with you going there?"

"Sir, I'm sorry," said Clarence, with a bit of a haughty air, "but was that a derogatory comment?"

Cunnyweather had completely lost the thread of the conversation. "Clarence?"

"Yes, sir?"

"Go back to work."

Roger Swinton returned from lunch to a mild disturbance in his cubicle. His ergonomic seat cushion had mysteriously disappeared. Puzzled, he searched his workstation for the wayward pillow. It was nowhere to be found. He popped his head over the divider wall. "Say, Clarence," he said, handily breaking the record for the most times he had addressed Clarence in a single month, much less a single day, "have you seen my cushion?" Clarence looked up from the report he was typing.

"No," he said, "I can't say that I have."

Roger, however, was unconvinced. "Really?" he prodded.

Clarence thought a little harder. "Yes," he said finally. "I'm sure. I haven't seen it." He resumed his typing.

"That's funny," interrupted Roger, "because it appears to be hidden under your shirt." And indeed, Clarence was sporting an ergonomic-seat-cushion-shaped hump on his back.

"What on earth are you talking about?" he asked, mildly offended.

"The seat cushion. The one under your shirt. Can I have it back, please?" demanded Roger, not entirely certain he *wanted* it back.

"Excuse me!" shouted Clarence, slamming his fist on the desk and jumping out of his chair. Everyone in a four-cubicle radius peeped over the walls at his exclamation. "How dare you accuse me of stealing your cushion! The object growing out of my back, if you must know, is a hump, and I use it for the long-term storage of water, and I would thank you very much not to draw attention to it, you God-awful bigot!" And he sat back down and resumed his typing.

Roger sat down at his own computer. He didn't want his cushion anymore.

At 4:00, Jane Tilfield, who worked at the other end of the floor, went to the water cooler for a quick drink. When she turned the corner, she stopped in her tracks, and her lip curled in mild disgust. Clarence had beaten her to the water and had pulled the five-gallon jug from its base. He was currently chugging as much of the spewing water as possible, the rest of it spilling on his pants and the carpeted floor. "Clarence!" Jane shouted. "What the hell is the matter with you?" Clarence lolled his eyes in her general direction but did not stop gorging himself on water. He did not speak until the last drop of water had spilled onto his upturned face.

"Storing water," Clarence gasped, out of breath. "Necessary for the desert." He stuck the empty jug back on its white stand and stalked back to his cubicle. As he passed her, he said, "Puh" and let fly a large glob of mucus that collided with Jane's thoroughly disgusted cheek.

At 4:30, Cunnyweather scratched his head. Never in his life had he received so many formal complaints from so many employees in one day. And they were all about the same employee. "Look," he said to the small crowd of people standing in his office. "Is all of this true?"

"It most certainly is!" gasped Jane Tilfield. "He drank all the water – every last drop! – and then… then, he *spat* on me!"

Roger Swinton nodded. "I saw it. And he stole my ergonomic seat cushion. He's been wearing it as a hump. I need that thing. I have scoliosis," he whined.

"He keeps asking me questions about Africa," said Joseph Demmelson miserably. "It's like, what? Because I'm black, I must know everything about Africa?"

Darleen Jukhov tapped her foot impatiently. "If he asks me one more time to climb on his back, I swear to God—"

Cunnyweather sighed. "All right, all right, I'll take care of it." He pushed through the small mob and out of his office. He marched down the aisle to Clarence's cubicle. He gave himself a rousing pep talk about the importance of good firing practices, a talk that usually helped in these circumstances. But when he entered Clarence's cubicle, it was empty. The computer had been turned off; all personal effects had been cleared from the desk. The entire area was neat and tidy, free of trash and dust, as if it hadn't been occupied for the last 15 years. The only evidence that someone had recently inhabited the cube was a small note taped to the computer monitor. Cunnyweather plucked it from the screen and studied it carefully. It was a drawing of a camel with a strangely human-like head, a head that donned the same style of glasses that Clarence did. It was signed, not with a name, but with a drawing that very closely resembled a hoof of some sort. And, strangest of all, there was a small trail of sand leading out of the cubicle. It led down the row, to the elevator at the end of the hall.

Because Clarence the camel didn't belong in a tiny cubicle working on the human grind. Clarence the camel had gone home.

The World, with Roger Blink

Transcript #926
Original broadcast date: 4/27/2024

Roger: This is Roger Blink with BBC World News, and I'm currently standing on Highland Street in Hempstead, and, as you can see, it is like every other street in the world at this time: lonely, dark, deserted, except for this house, here, across the street. The lamps in number 118 Highland still burn into the night, lighting an otherwise apocalyptically dark world for Ms. Miranda Bickle and her daughter, Potsie. These two ladies are, in fact, the last two people on Earth. What must it be like to know that you are the lone survivors in a world that's suffered absolutely catastrophic losses over the last three weeks? Billions upon billions have died or vanished; literally the entire population of the planet, save these two. Why? For what purpose? To what end? We aim to answer that question tonight, on *The World, with Roger Blink*.

[Cue "The World, with Roger Blink" theme music and opening montage.]

Roger: We are now standing directly outside the Bickle residence. As you can see, the house is very much being lived in, as we can tell by this rather fresh chalk drawing on the sidewalk leading up to the house. It appears to be a likeness of a woman with a finger up her nose, with the label, "Mommy is a poo-poo head." And an arrow, here, pointing back to the woman. Willful, childish spirit, we can see, has not diminished in the face of absolute tragedy. Bravo, little Potsie. Now let's see if we can speak to Ms. Bickle herself.

[Roger knocks on front door. Door opens.]

Roger: Hello, are you Miranda Bickle?

Miranda: Yes?

Roger: Hello, I'm Roger Blink, with BBC World News. You must recognize me from the telly.

Miranda: I've never heard of you!

Roger: Right, well, it's a confusing time for all of us, isn't it?

Miranda: Is it?

Roger: Yes, of course. Might we come in and have a few words with you?

Miranda: I guess you might as well do. I've just put the kettle on.

[Feet shuffling, door closing. Miranda's footsteps into the kitchen.]

Roger: Thank you so much. Is Potsie home as well?

Miranda: [Off camera, from the kitchen] Yes, she is, the little hell-scamp. Is that what this is about?

Roger: No, no. You see—

Miranda: [Off camera, from the kitchen] What's the little bugger done now?

Potsie: [Off camera, from elsewhere in the house] Mum!

Miranda: [Off camera, from the kitchen] What?!

Potsie: [**Off camera, from elsewhere in the house**] Don't call me a bugger!

Miranda: But darling, you *are* a bugger! Just a few more minutes on the tea, gentlemen.

Roger: No problem. I was wondering if we might—

Potsie: [**Off camera, from elsewhere in the house**] Am not!
Miranda: For Heaven's sake, Potsie, who isn't what?

Potsie: [**Off camera, from elsewhere in the house**] I am not a bugger!

Miranda: We've moved off that already!

Roger: Ms. Bickle, I was wondering if we might get little Potsie in here to join us.

Miranda: Heh. Your funeral, it is. Potsie! Front and center!

[Hurried footsteps down the hall.]

Potsie: I was drawing my pictures!

Miranda: Well, now you'll talk to this gentleman.

Potsie: This gentleman?

Miranda: Yes, young lady, this gentleman.

Potsie: This gentleman smells like burnt milk!

Roger: Ahh… Potsie, my name's Roger Blink, I'm with BBC World News. Would you mind if we asked you and your mum a few questions?

Potsie: Dunno.

Roger: Eloquently casual despite Armageddon. Pip, pip! Now, listen. Miranda. Potsie. As you know, having borne this whole "end of the world" business, you two are the last two people on earth. Give us your thoughts on that.

[**Several moments of silence.**]

Miranda: Beg pardon?

Roger: We would like your thoughts on what it's like to be the last two people on Earth.

Miranda: This is one of those hidden camera shows, I suppose?

Roger: Not at all! We're with the BBC World News! Am I—am I correct in understanding that you were unaware that you and Potsie are the last two people on earth?

Miranda: If it's true, no one told me.

Roger: Oh. Well, then. I feel a bit on the spot now, but… well, it's true. You see, you are, in fact, the last two people on earth. Everyone else – very literally everyone else – has perished in the unnatural blights we've experienced over the last three weeks and… you're sure no one mentioned this to you?

Miranda: Quite sure.

Roger: You haven't noticed the dead bodies in the streets? Didn't see the raging fires? Didn't feel the earthquakes? The plague, the famine, the—the zombies, and whatnot?

Miranda: I've been busy.

Roger: That is astonishing!

Miranda: I do macramé. It keeps me quite occupied.

Roger: Macramé?

Miranda: Owls, mostly.

[Miranda walks to the hall closet and opens the door. It is crammed full of macramé owls, many of which spill onto the floor.]

Roger: I see.

Miranda: So you're telling me every other sod in the whole world… all hundreds of people… all dead, except us?

Roger: Well, billions of people, actually. But yes, that's about where we stand, yes.

[Several moments of pause.]

Miranda: I guess I'll turn off the kettle then.
Potsie: It's not true! Binky hasn't died at all!

Roger: Binky? Who's Binky?

Potsie: My teddy!

Miranda: He's not a real person, you dolt!

Potsie: Oh yes he is! He loves me, and we're to be married! And he's not dead! I'll go fetch him.

[Potsie runs off down the hall.]

Roger: You see, Ms. Bickle, several worldwide agencies have conducted very specific tests with the most sensitive equipment, and all final tests show that everyone else on the planet is quite dead or else completely vanished. Only you and your daughter remain.

Miranda: Isn't that a fine how-do-you-do?

Roger: Now, I must ask you: first impressions?

Miranda: I won't have to call my mum anymore.

Roger: Yes, I suppose that's true.

Miranda: But I'll have to fetch my own milk now, won't I?

Roger: Quite so.

Miranda: That's a wank.

Roger: A "wank," yes. Now, Ms. Bickle, what will you do? Obviously, repopulation is quite out of the question.

Miranda: Oh, quite! Potsie's a nightmare; I'll never make that mistake again.

Roger: So, what will you do now that everyone else is gone?

Miranda: Well. I guess I'll turn the guest room into a pantry.

Roger: I suppose that would be more practical now.

Miranda: Or maybe a breakfast nook. I've always wanted a breakfast nook.

[Potsie returns from her room.]

Potsie: You see? He's fine!

Roger: This is Binky?

Potsie: Yes.

Roger: His eye's fallen off!

Potsie: He's just misplaced it!

Roger: He doesn't look fine to me.

Miranda: Potsie, dear, why won't you play with Binky in the breakfast nook?

Potsie: We don't have a breakfast nook.

Miranda: We do now!

Roger: I must say, you seem to be taking this news with aplomb.

Miranda: We don't eat plums. Never trusted 'em. Never will.

Roger: No, *aplomb*. It means with great composure. You're taking this
news with great composure.

Miranda: How should I take it?

Roger: Oh, I don't know. Shock? Fear? Distress?

Miranda: Because the people are gone?

Roger: Yes.

Miranda: I don't like most people.
Roger: I see. But what will you do for food? For nourishment? Clothing, transportation, *et cetera, et cetera*?

Miranda: We've still got stores, haven't we? Buildings haven't died off, have they?

Roger: Well, no, I mean, technically stores do exist, but—

Miranda: Then I expect we'll be fine.

Roger: But there won't be people to manage them. Don't you see? No one to manufacture the clothes, or grow the food, or process the toilet tissue, or any of it. No one to stock the shelves.

Miranda: No one to stock the shelves! You ain't been to our market, have you? Won't be much of a change, there. Those stock boys were always lazy buggers.

Potsie: [Off camera, from elsewhere in the house] Stop calling me a bugger!

Miranda: I'm not calling you a bugger, I'm calling the stock boys at the market buggers!

Potsie: [Off camera, from elsewhere in the house] Who?

Miranda: The stock boys at the market!

Potsie: [Off camera, from elsewhere in the house] Oh! They *are* buggers!

Miranda: Watch your language! Now, gentlemen, I'll have to ask you to leave. I've got to get Potsie ready—she has a play date with Janie down the street.

Roger: Have you listened to anything I've said?

Miranda: Yes, of course.

Roger: Janie's quite dead, you understand that. Her face is likely melted into some puddle in the street.

Miranda: No reason to be rude, though, is it? The Bickles never miss an appointment. Potsie! Get your boots on! It looks like rain!

Roger: Looks like rain? Madame, it looks like hellfire and brimstone!

Miranda: Best grab your slicker as well!

Roger: Well... there you have it. Miranda Bickle and Potsie Bickle: the last two survivors on this planet. Yet, they... they face the disastrous future with... with courage, and with grace.

Miranda: Hurry up, you bugger, it's time for mummy's medication!

[Miranda slips a flask out of her apron pocket and winks at the camera.]

Potsie: [Off camera, from elsewhere in the house] Hold off a bit! I've got to take a leak!

Roger: For the BBC—

Potsie: [Off camera, from elsewhere in the house] Mum, I've got stuck in my trousers!

Miranda: For Heaven's sake, Potsie! Do you want to play with Janie or not?

Potsie: [Off camera, from elsewhere in the house] Mum, is Janie dead?

Miranda: What's that got to do with anything?

Roger: This has been *The World, with Roger Blink*. Back to BBC World News.

[Cue "The World, with Roger Blink" theme music and closing montage.]

About the Author

Photo by Emily Rose Studios

Clayton Smith is a sometimes-writer, sometimes-napper based in Chicago, where he uses neither his bachelor's in journalism nor his master's in arts management. He is often calamitous, and good at bacon. He lives with his impressively tolerant wife.

Clayton's other works include *Apocalypticon* and the comedic play *Death and McCootie*, which debuted at the 2013 New York International Fringe Festival.

 @Claytonsaurus

 facebook.com/Claytonsaurus

Made in the USA
Charleston, SC
14 May 2014